LOVE & FIRE

BOOK ONE

BY KARLEE N. CLEVERLEY

DORRANCE PUBLISHING CO
EST. 1920
PITTSBURGH, PENNSYLVANIA 15238

Dorrance Publishing Co
585 Alpha Drive
Suite 103
Pittsburgh, PA 15238
Visit our website at *www.dorrancebookstore.com*

ISBN: 979-8-8852-7130-1
eISBN: 979-8-8852-7857-7

LOVE & FIRE

BOOK ONE

PROLOGUE

I lay in my makeshift nest that I made out of boredom. I melted obsidian to form a bowl-like shape for the nest. Although, I might as well have made it out of a volcano for all of the obsidian it used. I also decorated it with natural rubies and topaz. It took a lot of experiments to get them to grow on the obsidian nest- not like I did not have the time. "Rubestia, come here for a moment," Mom calls from the castle. I'm often uncomfortable there. Since I have no human form, I often change my size to that of a smaller bird like a macaw; however, I look the same as before. I stare at my far wall made of half silver and half iron. Most humans would see this as a mirror. I, however, have no means to burn sand. Okay, burning sand to glass is very easy for me, I just can't make it into a modern mirror. So, I Improvised with silver, and since silver is fairly soft, I mixed it with iron to harden it. I also took ten years to polish it, so it's now very reflective. The wall is about eight feet tall by twenty feet long. I've never really measured it. It's not like I really can measure it, being a bird and all.

I lift my head up. Although there are no lights in this cave, my feathers give off a faint glow. I stare into my mirror, even though I've seen myself many times. The unusual white feathers still baffle me. I'm mainly white with royal gold as my second color. The gold is on my Remiges (commonly known as flight feathers) and on my rectrices (tail feathers). I also have five very long, flexible feathers that are white and thin until you get to the end, which is puffy and gold. I have two on my head, which make me look like I have antennas, and three on my tail. I also have a gold diamond shape on my forehead or, as my clan calls it, the mark of the queen. I have tiny gold feathers at the end of my eyes, which make my eyes look like they're on fire when lit. Only my gold feathers burn; my white feathers only ever burn if it is for me to shift.

I close my eyes, which are blue by the way. Instead of the black dot humans call an iris, I have a flame that never gives out. I'm about to fall asleep when I hear a summons from the castle. I stand up, glance at my nest, ruffle my feathers, and walk to the edge of the cave. I jump off, letting the air catch my wings. I drift down for a moment before flying up to the castle. I fly over the town, and many citizens wave up at me. I love my phoenix clan, and we also have other races mixed in with us. I know there are at least twenty dragons here and there, as well as thirteen griffins. We also have humans, but don't be fooled into thinking that there are a lot. There are only about six humans at the moment. Most are actually male phoenixes. Since they are unable to shift into a bird, they look human, but they do have differences.

Male phoenixes are born with the ability to control fire. They also have at least three feathers on their brows, though they can have a whole head of feathers like my brother Jasper. I fly through the window of the throne room. The only part of the castle that doesn't have glass is the windows. Flames cover my body as I shift my form to the size of a macaw and land on my brother Carter's shoulder, since he is the closest to the window. He pats my head and turns to our mom and dad, who are sitting on their thrones. "Good, you are all here now. I wish to discuss the trip to the dragon kingdom to the east," Mom says, tapping the arm of her chair. I've met the dragon royalty a few times. I guess it's time for a meeting with them. We do it about every twenty years. I feel the fire within me burn hotter than it has ever been before. It is so hot that it actually hurts. I fall off my brother's shoulder and onto the ground. He quickly goes and picks me up.

I suddenly burst into flames, startling my brother even though the flames won't harm him. I feel a flutter of giddiness and pure joy, as well as a tug toward the north. As if possessed, I launch myself toward the window as fast as I can. I faintly hear my family calling out to me, but something is driving me toward the north. I fly as fast as I am able to, the joy becoming stronger the closer I get to wherever it is that's calling me. In the thousand years I've been alive,

I've never felt this alive. Soon, my flames become so bright with my joy that they are now white. I land on a tree near a large open space within the forest. I smell wolves; I look around and there are no wolves out at the moment. The same tugging sensation is pulling me toward the large home that is surrounded by smaller ones. I fly off the branch and fly toward the home, following the tugging wherever it takes me. I soon feel it tug me toward a small window. I focus on dimming my fires so as not to alarm any onlookers.

I gently land on the windowsill. It's a fairly large room, I suppose. I see a lady lying on the bed; she looks to be in pain, even though relief and joy are on her face. There is also a man, but his back is facing me. Soon, I see a man in a green garb walk in with a white bundle. He hands the bundle to the lady lying in a bed with the man holding her hand. The lady has tears running down her face. The man lets go of the lady's hand so that she may hold the bundle. I'm not sure why the bundle is so interesting to me. I don't know what it is until the lady turns toward the man to show him. I now know that the bundle is actually a baby. I look at the baby and my inner flames roar to life, wild and free. I know that this baby is my mate. I watch the family kiss and hold their child. Soon, the man in green garb comes in with a plastic container with a lamp. He takes my mate and lies him on it. He then attaches things onto my mate. I'm not sure what they are, but the parents don't seem to be worried and my mate does not seem to be in pain. I calm down and wait until nightfall.

As they fall asleep, the man is holding the lady in his arms. They are both smiling in their sleep. I melt the glass and fly in. I land on the edge of the plastic container. The plastic cuts into my feet since it's so thin. I ignore it and look at the little bundle of a mate. A werewolf? I don't recall there ever being a werewolf as a phoenix mate. Nevertheless, I accept him wholeheartedly. I turn to my future in-laws, and then I quickly turn back to my mate as I feel something touch my left talon. My mate is awake and looking at me. The sudden urge to take him away and protect him comes over me. I shake my head and ruffle my feathers. That's a very bad idea, as I have no means to care for a child, let alone one that will be my mate. However, I will be able to protect him from afar with my mark. I open my beak and puncture the flashy spot between his neck and shoulder. My flames brighten on impact, and he cries out as a piece of my inner flame enters him. "I will be waiting for you, my mate." I say when the mark is halfway done. It will be complete when he marks me as his mate. I quickly fly out before his parents hear his cry and wake up.

I land on the windowsill and turn my head to see my mate one more time. He is still crying, even though I know the wound is fully healed. "I'm sorry, mate, I did not mean to scare you," I say to myself. I see the man stir and get up. He walks to my mate and picks him up. He kisses his forehead and rocks him to sleep. I know no blood is shed, as my inner flame will heal as soon as it enters his body. I cannot wait to get my human form and then meet him once more. I turn my head and fly home in joy, spinning in circles and chirping happily.

Last Day of School

"Asland Mark Johnson. Get your furry rear end out of bed!" I groan as I push against my bed. I pull the covers off and stretch. I get out of bed and walk into my bathroom. I look into the mirror; my brown hair is a complete mess. My sea green eyes are slightly closed because of the bright lights of my bathroom. There is also a large burn mark on the base of my neck where my left shoulder meets it. Mom says I had it since I was born, even though there was no fire near me during that time, not even a candle. I comb through my hair and brush my teeth. As you heard my mom yell, I'm Asland Mark Johnson. I'm seventeen, though I'll be turning eighteen tomorrow. I'm also the son of the alpha of the Firestorm Pack. Oh, did I forget to mention that I am a werewolf? Well I am, and since I'm the son of the alpha, I got my wolf form at the tender age of eight instead of sixteen like other wolves. Eight is even early for an alpha wolf to become a wolf.

However, I will still be unable to find my mate until I'm sixteen. I've been looking for her for two years now. I turn off the water and walk back into my room. As I get dressed, mom yells from downstairs, "Breakfast is done!" I smile at the mention of food. I run down the stairs, two at a time. I quickly enter the kitchen and run to the food. I hear my mom's soft laughter. I turn toward her and gave her a toothy grin. She returns my smile with her own. "Boys and their food," she says. She turns back and starts cooking again. Every member of the pack tributes to the pack in their own way; even the pups try to help, which is way too cute. My mom is the luna of the pack, which is the female alpha. There are natural born female alphas, though they are very rare and their mates are called lunas. The luna helps the alpha with the pack by assigning tasks and help keep the peace. When the luna is happy, the pack is happy. If she is sad, so is the pack. If she is hurt, well.... RUN!

I look at the time and see that it's time for school. I wolf down my pancakes and bacon. I grab my bag and keys and run to the garage. I get into my black Toyota Camry and race off as soon as the garage door is open. The drive to school is a long one; in fact, it is only six thirty in the morning and school starts at eight. I roll down my windows so the forest scent fills my car. The pack members all have jobs in human society. Since we live much longer than humans, we gain a lot more knowledge over time than they do, though they learn so much quicker than us since they know that their lives are so short. No, humans don't know we exist, nor do they know about the others that live with them, such as vampires. Contrary to popular belief, werewolves and vampires don't hate each other. We actually have a coven nearby. They also have a heart beat as well as heat. There are dragon sifters as well as cats. Now, that's a love-hate relationship there.

I soon pull into the school parking lot with time to spare. I park my car in an empty space and cut the engine. I get out and head to the torture chamber they call school. "Land!" I growl as I hear the stupidest nickname ever. I continue walking, not acknowledging my best friend and soon to be beta. He runs up to me and puts his arms around my shoulders. He's a little smaller than my six foot one. "Mitch, get your arm off or lose it," I growl with the hint of playfulness. Mitchell sighs as he pulls his arm away. "As violent as ever, I see." I roll my eyes and head to my locker. "So, I hear you're having a party tomorrow for your birthday."

"Yeah, you're the one that's planning it," I say as I put my stuff away and grab what I need for class. I close my locker and head to class when I hear the most awful thing ever. "Babes!" A high pitch screeching voice calls out. I growl and continue to walk to class. "Babes wait up!" I hear her running in her high heels, so I do the most logical thing and walk faster. Mitchell runs to class, leaving me to fend for myself. Just as I'm about to enter the classroom, a claw-like hand grabs my shirt. "Babes, why do you keep running from me?" I turn and glare at her. Two months before my sixteenth birthday, Amnia shifted into her wolf form. Ever since then, she has been clinging onto me and saying that we're mates.

At first, I was flattered but when she went to kiss me, Claude, my wolf spirit, growled in anger. That's when I knew she was lying about being my mate, but I had no proof so I put my trust in Claude and stayed away from her. Ever since then, I've smelt different men on her. Which disgusted me; if she was truly my mate she would've waited for two months to prove her statement, not turn around and go dating every desperate unmated male within the pack. However, this school is neutral territory, so there are four different packs coming to here. Now that I have my wolf form, I definitely know for a fact that she is not my mate, though she still acts like she is. "Come on, we're mates," she begs. Claude growls and takes over. He grabs onto her neck and pushes her against the wall. His claws do not break skin but are very close to it. "You. Are. Not. My. Mate." He growls out every word deadlier than the last. "Even if you were, I would have hoped you would have waited two months to prove your statement, then to go dating every desperate unmated male out there. I smell them all over you and it's disgusting. Fortunately, I'm now almost eighteen and can tell that you are not my mate." He releases her and hands me back control. I walk into class and sit down. I ignored the stares; luckily, she didn't make me late to class. I can't wait to find my mate, my one and only. I hope my mate is kind and fights for what she believes in.

"And don't forget beautiful," Claude says as he puts in his two cents. "I'm more into her personality than her looks; looks are just a bonus," I think. I sense Claude nod in agreement since he's only the spirit of his old self. Every werewolf gets the wolf spirit of a past wolf. The spirit wolves are guides into the wolf world. They usually take most of the pain of the first shift. They are also the ones that help us find our soul mates. We can find them ourselves, but our wolves can find them faster. No, our bodies don't break apart and reform after every shift. That's only for the first shift. After that, our body just goes into a different dimension while we are in our wolf forms, so we still have our clothes and items from before. We just switch bodies back and forth. It's mandatory to switch at least one day a week at most to care for the other body or it will be like the first shift all over again.

We are also very protective and possessive of our mates. Male or female- it doesn't matter to us, especially to alpha male wolves. It's just in our nature.

Though we learn to control this so that it's not over the top and ruling over us. I just can't wait until we find my mate. "Asland!" yells Mitchell. I look up at my friend. "What?" He crosses his arms. "Class is over and I've called you like five times. The next class is about to start." Claude starts laughing at me, which sounds like a choking dog. I grab my bag and run to my next class. Great, I haven't met my mate and she already consumes my mind.

The bell rings right as my foot enters the class. "Cutting it a bit close there, Mr. Johnson." I give Mrs. Wrish a smile. She is one of my favorite teachers. She's a tiny and sweet old Native American lady with kind brown eyes as well as a gray cloud for hair, but do not get on her bad side. She can be scary, even though she's just a human. She returns my smile, "Well, take your seat." I walk to my desk and sit down. Fortunately, it's the last day of school until summer break. Why am I at school? For the class parties, of course, although not all of the classes are doing them.

"Everyone to the gym for yearbook signing," the loud speakers announce. I decide to just head home. I bolt to my car before that witch comes and asks me to sign her yearbook. Though I can't outrun her forever, since she is part of my pack. I get to my car and get in. Just as I start the engine, someone decides to jump onto my trunk. I let out a growl as Mitchell gets off. "Hey, can I hitch a ride?" I smile, "Sorry. Only babes can hitch a ride in my car." Mitch gives me a fake shock look while having his hand over his heart. "Who are you, and what have you done to my sweet Land?" I growl at the nickname. "Get in before I leave." Mitchell hops in, and I drive out of the school parking lot. "Can we go get something to eat before getting home?" I roll my eyes. "He loves food even more than you do," Claude says to me. I grin at this comment.

We pull into a Wendy's drive through. "Welcome to Wendy's, order when you are ready." I look at the menu and nothing looks very good. "I'll have a large chocolate Frosty and my friend will have a large Baconator meal with a large fry and Coke." Mitchell has a large grin. "Oh buddy, that smile is leaving soon," I think. "Oh, you know me so well, I could kiss you," Mitch teases as he grins. "One, that's gross, and two, you're paying," I say with a hint of playfulness. Mitch's face falls because he hates paying. I hear a soft laugh on the intercom. "A large chocolate Frosty, a large Baconator with a large fry, and a Coke, is that correct?" The girl's voice is squeaky because of the intercom.

"Yes," I say as the girl gives me the price and tells me it will be the second window. I pull up to the window. Mitch hands me his money. The girl slides the window open, I hand her the money, and she gives back the change. After a minute, she comes back with the food. I drive off with a pouting Mitchell since I don't allow eating in my car.

After we get home, I eat my Frosty while Mitch stuffs his face. We decide to play Call of Duty. I dominate the game. "Boys, dinner's done," I hear mom call out. "Race ya," Mitch says as he already runs off. "Oh, you're on." I call back and sprint past him. He growls in frustration. As I'm running, my baby sister Lilly walks out of the bathroom. "Lilly, grab your brother!" Michell yells. "Oh resorting to little pups, now are we?" I think. Lilly loves to try and stop me whenever Mitchell and I race. She jumps forward into my path. I'm prepared for it and scoop her into my arms as I continue to run. "I win," I call out as I enter the room. I sit Lilly in her highchair, which already has a plate of food on it. I serve myself a plate and sit down next to Dad. After dinner, I head up to my room and take a shower. Tomorrow's my birthday party. "Yeah, and let's hope our mate is there," Claude howls in joy. "Well," I tell him, "let's get to bed so the morning can come faster." I get into my pajama pants and get under my blankets. "Good night, Claude." I close my eyes as I hear him say good night.

FIRE

I am walking in unfamiliar woods; even the scent is strange. Where am I? I hear a twig snap close by. Soon, a jet-black wolf the size of a horse comes out. Its gold eyes stare at me. "Claude, is that you?" The wolf nods, "Yes, Asland." Wait, why can I see him? Is this a dream? "You're half right. It's not reality but not a dream either. I pulled your spirit into the spirit realm because I had to tell you something." I look at Claude; he is a great looking wolf.

What? This is the first time I've really got to see what my wolf form looks like. "And this couldn't wait until morning?" I ask. Claude shakes his massive head. "I sense danger coming." In the far distance, I hear a strange noise like an alarm. Did I forget to turn off my alarm clock? "That's no alarm clock," Claude states, and that's when I figure it out. It is the attack alarm. "Claude return me to my body, I have to fight." Claude nods, and everything starts to fade away.

I open my eyes and jump out of bed. I run to my window to see a whole pack of rouges attacking. I quickly run out of my room and down the stairs. I'm on the verge of shifting as I take the stairs two at a time, though they are wide enough for a wolf. The last time I ran down the stairs in wolf form was when I was ten. I ended up on my head. I swore to myself never to run down the stairs as a wolf again. As soon as I touch the first floor, I let the shifting take hold. I run through the already busted doors. I then launch myself into the battle. I'm instantly surrounded by four rouges. Their eyes are bloodshot with no sign of their former selves. Their fur is matted with dirt and blood. I stand my ground and let out a growl. The four of them go in for the attack. I instantly have one by the throat, as two jump onto my back and the other bites my forepaw. I hit the wolf that bit me with the wolf that is now dead. Then, I roll to get the other two off me. They jump off and land just as I get back onto my feet.

I stand with my head up, ignoring the wounds on my back and paw. The three rogues growl at me, and I growl back. "They seem to be way too organized, and there are way too many of them for this to be a normal attack," Claude says. Although I do not look away from the three rogues, I know that Claude is right. Someone has to be organizing this attack, but for what reason? The three attack, and then two of them are attacked by Mitchell and John, who is my delta. I quickly deal with my attacker. Soon ,the rogues retreats and we check our wounds. We didn't lose anyone or we would have felt it within the bond. I see my father's large gray wolf figure lift his head in a victory howl. I lift my own head and howl with him. The rest of the pack joins in. After the howl, many of the less injured wolves took care of the bodies as my father calls his beta and delta to his side. Mine come to my side, even though I didn't call them. "Happy eighteenth birthday to you, man," Mitch says sarcastically through the mind-link. "Just so you know. I did not invite the four rogues to the party," Mitch jokes though the mind-link. "Dude, shut up," John mind-links back.

"Asland, come to my office with your beta and delta," Dad mind-links me privately. "Come on you two, the Alpha wants us in the office." I link the two of them and head back to the house. As we reach the house, we shift back into our human forms. The office is on the seventh floor, and I often wish we had an elevator, although this pack house has been made long before elevators. We soon get to my father's office. I knock on the doors, and my dad's voice calls out, "Come in, son." I enter with Mitchell and John behind me. Mitchell sits by his dad, who's my father's delta. Unlike the alpha position that is inherited, the beta and delta are callings, and the alphas share some of their power with them. I sit down on the seat closest to my father. John is next to his uncle, the beta. "The rogues were way too many in number and way too organized for this to be a random attack," the Delta says as he hits the table.

"Calm down, Mark," Dad says calmly, though he is anything but calm. "Alpha, do you think he's back?" the beta asks, and Mark pales instantly. Dad sighs, "Oh God. I hope not." I look at my beta and delta. They look just as confused as me. We turn back to the alpha. "Dad, who's back?" My father looks at me. "Kaleb M. Johnson, who now calls himself Alpha Jackson," he says, just as the Delta scoffs "alpha, my butt." My dad looks at Mark, and he bows his head slightly at my father. "Who is Kaleb?" I ask; I still don't understand why this guy is so important. "He is my older brother." My eyes widen at my father's words. "I did not see that coming!" Claude says in surprise. "Neither did I," I reply back to him. My father continues, "Though the Alpha position is normally given to the first born, my father gave me the title instead."

"Your brother may have had the power of an alpha, but he did not have the heart of one," the beta says while looking at my father. The meeting continues for about an hour or two over the plans to prepare the pack in case it really was Kaleb who organized the attack with the four rogues. As soon as the meet is over, Mitchell puts a blindfold over my eyes. He then puts my arms behind my back and holds my wrists with one hand. Though I can easily get out, I let him take me. He guides me down the stairs. Soon, I can smell the crisp scent of the pines outside. I also start to hear music. I'm not sure if we are on the first floor or outside. I stumble over the stairs. Mitchell quickly catches me and helps me get my balance back. The music is live; there's no soft undertone of the electronics. The music gets louder with each step. I soon go up a few stairs and the music stops. Mitchell releases my hands and takes the blindfold off. I'm on the stage that my father uses when he makes a pack announcement.

The pack is looking up at me with smiles; many already healed from the battle early this morning. A few are still healing, and I know my back is still healing. My right hand that was bitten is now healed. Most, if not all, supernatural creatures heal very quickly, some faster than others. Werewolves are on the lower end of the healing speed. Witches and witch doctors are the closest to humans in lifespans and healing speed, though their healing is still faster than that of humans. I look around and see that a few of the neighboring packs and the nearby coven are here. "Well, what are we waiting for? Let's get this party started!" I shout and jump down from the stage. I stand straight, ignoring the throbbing pain from my back I talk to a lot of vampires, as well as to the members of the other packs.

I dance with a few girls and didn't care whether they were vampire or wolf. I refused Amia multiple times, and she didn't take it well each time. I dance with my baby sister, though dancing with her is just her standing on my feet as I dance. We then have an early dinner, since the battle with the rouges took over our time for breakfast and lunch. The cake was amazing after dinner. The whole party was a blast and soon everyone returns home or to their rooms. I stay and try to help clean up after the party. After being told ten times that I must leave, I give up and head to my room. Thoroughly exhausted, I fall onto my bed and crash.

"Come," the most entrancing voice says as it enters my mind. "Come to me, my Love." I open my eyes and see fire everywhere. "Crap!" I open my window and remember that I'm on the eighth floor. "Crap!" Panic starts to take hold of my heart. I turn and run out of my room and through the flames. I jump down the stairs and over fallen objects. I also dodge falling objects. After five floors and many close calls, I decide now was the time to jump or I would burn alive. I run to the nearest window and jump through it. The glass cuts me on my arms and legs. Once my feet hit the ground, I immediately drop and roll in the grass to get the fire off me.

I soon feel something drop onto my shoulders. I look and see it is a blanket. I wrap it around me. "My baby!" I hear my mom cry as she wraps her arms around me. "Doctor, come check my son." I feel my adrenaline start to settle down. I know that the cuts are already gone because of our fast healing as werewolves. "Okay, move out of the way. An old man is coming through." The doctor comes closer with a wet cloth and starts to clean the black ashes off me. Soon, the doctor's eyes are full of shock and disbelief.

"What's wrong?" I ask, starting to panic again. The doctor quickly let go of my arm as though it burned him. "Nothing, that's what's wrong. You have no burns. You were covered in ash but no burns. Also, just then, when you asked what was wrong, your skin heated up and burned me." To prove his point, he shows his right hand that had held my arm. It is red and blistering. I look at my arms and legs and realize that what the doctor said is in fact true. I have no burns. Mitch comes into view, "Lucky you. I got my shoulder burned. It'll take three hours to heal."

As everyone settles down, my father pulls me aside. "Son, are you okay? You look like you're in a daze." I nod. All I can think about is that voice. Dad nods back and calls in the pack. "Everyone, we are going to the Moonlit pack for shelter. Do not fear for we have land and a pack house for us. It's a far journey there, but the land is bigger and more beautiful than it is here. There are also homes for those who don't wish to be in the pack house. It will still be a rule for all eighteen-year olds to move into the pack house until mated.

We will be getting supplies for the journey after we get to the Moonlit Pack. We will also visit other packs to get more supplies. This is a three-week journey. Those who don't wish to do the journey, the Moonlit pack have agreed to let you join their pack. You can sleep on it before you make your decision." With that, we head to the Moonlit pack. Many of us were in our wolf forms. Those who don't have a wolf form are riding on their parent's or older sibling's backs. Once we get to the Moonlit territory, my father howls. We wait for the Moonlit pack to howl back to let us into their pack's territory. We receive the howl and enter the territory.

We enter and head to the pack house. It soon comes into sight. The wolves nod to us with looks of sympathy. I bite back a growl as Claude gets angry. Their alpha comes and greets us. "Hello, Firestorm Pack. We have the guest rooms ready, but we're afraid that many of you may not have beds and for that we are sorry." My father shifts to talk to their alpha. "That is all right; we will be leaving at noon. You have given us more than we could ask for."

The Moonlit Alpha nods and smiles as his luna comes out. "Welcome, we're so sorry about your pack house." I feel the pack's sadness with the pack mind-link. "Come, we'll show you to your rooms." The pack breaks into groups as guides are assigned to show them where they will stay for the night. The Moonlit Alpha has us follow him to our room. Each family will be getting a single room for the night, which means that I'll be sharing a room with my mom, dad, and baby sister Lilly. My parents get the bed and my sister and I get the couch. "Hey, it's better than the floor," Claude says to me. I nod in agreement. Mom hands me a pillow and blanket. "Will you be okay, Bear?"

"Hey, it's better than the floor," I copy Claude and give her a warm smile. Mom laughs, and she pulls my head down and kisses my forehead. "Goodnight, bear." Don't ask me about the nickname. "Good night, Mom." She walks over to the bed and gets in. I put the pillow on the couch. I wrap the blanket around me and lie down on the couch. As I close my eyes, I'm met with the events of last night: fire everywhere, alarms blasting, and the voice asking me to find her.

Starting the Journey

I'm woken up by my sister jumping on me. I growl and open my eyes. I tell her to head on over to breakfast. I mind-link mom that I'll be taking a shower and ask her if I can get some clothes. I hear a knock on the door to the bathroom. "I'm Arron. Luna asked me to bring you some clothes. I've set them next to the door," he says before walking away. I finish showering, and then I open the door and see a pile of clothes. I pick them up and close the door. I put the clothes on; the shirt is a little small on me, but all the rest of the clothes fit. I follow the smell of food to the kitchen.

"Welcome, come eat, we made extra for all of you," the Moonlit Luna smiles as I walk in. I see our pack already eating. As I get my food, my father clears his throat. This is never a good sign. "My dear pack, I trust that you had a good night's sleep. I must ask again, who is willing to go on this journey? You have until noon to decide." I wonder how many are going to leave. "I don't want to think about it," Claude says bitterly. in other words, he just told me to shut up. After eating, I walk out of the pack house and look toward the woods. I notice that many of the Moonlit Pack are gathering up supplies for us, although we don't need many thing since many of us can hunt for food to eat or be in our wolf forms and sleep outside. I sit down on the steps. I soon feel a hand onto my shoulder. "Son, do you wish to stay here?" As soon as my dad asks, the mysterious voice replays in my head. "No, I will go," I say with no hesitation. My father gives me a nod with no emotion, but I know that he is glad I chose to go.

Soon, noon has arrived and everything is ready. The bags are made for our wolves. Those who have children under sixteen are allowed one to two tents. Many of the men carried the bags and tents. There are also carts for those who can't shift. They are attached to the bags. Since Lilly is the only one that can't shift in our family, she'll ride on mom's back. Since she is only five, we have one tent for her and our parents. We also won't have a cart. "Asland, you're carrying the bag for our family." I nod at dad's command through the mind-link.

I shift, and one of the male wolves of the Moonlit Pack sets a bag onto my back with a tent. Two girls from my pack come over. They are under fifteen, so they are in charge of unbuckling us. The man shows them how. I growl because the man decides to use me as an example and makes the buckle too tight. Then, he makes it too loose, which throws me off balance. Now, he shows the girls how to properly find out how tight it should fit. Once he is done, the girls headed off to go do the buckles. "Sorry about that, boy," says the man.

I growl at his words, and I guess my power slips into the growl. "Oh, you must be the alpha's son Asland. I'm Jack, and I'm joining you guys with my mate and kids." I nod and walk away. It feels weird having something on my back. This must be what a horse feels like. "Don't compare us to a horse!" Claude growls at me. I roll my eyes and glance around. There are around fifty wolves and athirty cildren. Once everything is done, we head off. Dad puts Lilly onto mom's back before shifting. Let's just say it takes a long time to do so since she always wants to ride on my back but I rarely let her. I also have the family bag full of clothes, blankets, water, and snacks. There are ten wolves that are carrying pots, pans, knives, and water. We have a lot of spices and dried fruits for when we can hunt for our family for meat. I follow behind my father and mom.

Three members choose to stay behind since their mates are in the Moonlit Pack and five members join us. Jack, his mate, and their three kids. We are now heading toward the Bloodstone Pack camp, which will take us a week to get to before we will be able to refill supplies. I look up at the sky through the tree leaves. "Aszy, can I get a snack?" asks my little sister. I look at Lilly, and then I trot up to my mom. Lilly digs into the side pocket for the snacks. It doesn't matter which side she digs into, since both sides are full of snacks and water. After hours of walking and many games of I Spy with Lilly, I just happen to drag Mitchell into playing the game until the sun starts to set.

"Let's call it a night," Dad mind-links to the pack. We find a small clearing with enough room for the tents for those who can't yet shift. The kids start to unbuckle their parents and the others. Soon, a boy named Jimmy comes and unbuckles me. As soon as the buckles are off, I let the stuff fall off my back. I know there's nothing in there that will break. We will only be setting up ten tents for all those who can't shift to sleep; everyone else will sleep in their wolf forms. It is both for protection and because there is barely enough room for ten tents. I lie down, but I have yet to shift. I am assigned to night watch on the perimeters. While the tents are being put up, I decide to take a nap. I close my eyes about to go to sleep when I feel a tiny body attempt to climb on my back. I open my eyes to see Lilly. "What do you want, Lilly?" I ask nicely through the mind-link. "Mommy told me to get you for dinner." I nod, "Okay, slide off so I can shift."

She slides off and turns back to me. I shift and follow her to the tent that my parents and sister share with two teenage girls. I sit down, and mom hands me a bowl of soup. The soup has the elk we hunted as we searched for a place to camp. We got three elks to feed the pack, so we only have enough to feed us for today. We are a fairly large pack. It is a bit strange for a large pack to travel together. I remember a meeting with my dad on my sixteenth birthday. He had a map on the wall and handed me a dart. He had me throw it at the map. I still have yet to figure out why. I get up to get myself another bowl. "Asland, come here for a moment," Mitchell says through the mind-link. I finish off my third bowl, and then I hand it to an elder lady who is assigned to wash the dishes. I smile at her and the others helping her as well. I go in search of Mitchell to see what he wants. I quickly find him with John. They are by themselves with a small campfire. "What do you want, my shift is about to start?" I ask him. "It will be really quick," Mitchell says, while John looks like he's about to be sick.

I look at both of them in confusion. Mitchell smiles at me with his "please don't kill me later" look. I'm instantly on guard; that look leads to more trouble than it's worth. Mitchell nods to John, who is as pale white as a sheet of paper. What on earth are they planning? They walk toward me, but I stay put trying to figure out what they're up to. Each of them grabs one of my arms and starts pulling me toward the fire. I'm beyond confused as to what they are doing, right up until they push me into the fire. My heart races in panic until the fire starts to sway like enchanted snakes. Soon the panic turns into anger, "You two are so dead," I growl. They immediately turn and run. I give chase all the way back to camp and tackle the two to the ground. I hold them both down with a hand. John is completely still while Mitchell tries to free himself. "I expected as much from Mitchell, but I didn't see you in the equation at all, John." He whimpers; though he has a soft heart and doesn't like fighting, he is very good at it. He will be a great delta for me and Mitchell, even though he loves to act like a fool. "I'm sorry, I didn't want to but Mitchell wanted to see if it was true," John says with a whimper.

"I know, but you still are going to be punished for helping him." He whimpers again with a "Yes, Alpha." "Now, Mitchell Ray Markson," I say. Mitchell freezes at the sound of his full name and mumbles under his breath, "I'm in for it now." I grab their shirts and pull them up. "John, go help with the dishes, and you are to finish them with no help. I'll link the pack so that they do not help you. As for you, Mitchell, you are to clean up the camp tomorrow morning as well as set it up without help." They both sigh, "Yes, Alpha." I let go of them and walk back to the edge of camp and shift into my wolf form. I quickly link the pack to the punishment for John and Mitchell as well as the reason why.

"Claude, you've been very quiet today," I say to my spirit wolf. "So?" Claude replies. I roll my eyes and head to my shift until another member comes to take my place. After about two hours, Kayia, an older she-wolf, comes to take over. I nod to her and head to camp. I lay under a nearby tree and fall asleep. I wake up to things moving. I stand up and shake the dirt off. I walk toward the camp. Mom was making breakfast. "Oh, good morning, Bear." I shift and hug her. "Morning," I looked for my dad in the camp but didn't see him. "Where's Dad?"

"I don't know, Bear." I nod and walked around to see if I can find him. "Hey, 'Land." I turn and see Mitchell with his three younger brothers and sister. "Hey, Mitch." I walk over to them. "Your dad said we're leaving after breakfast." I nod and then ask, "Speaking of my dad, do you know where he is?" Mitchell shakes his head. I sigh. I don't even know why I'm looking for him. "Maybe to see if there's something that you can do?' Claude suggests;

this sounds about right. I'm about to continue my search when I remember Mitchell's punishment, "Oh, by the way, have fun cleaning up camp." Mitchell groans in response. I smile and walk off. I soon find my dad back with my mom and Lilly. "Oh, hey son." He greets me as he sees me.

"I was wondering what I could do to help?" He stops to think. "Well, we need a pair of wolves to go scouting ahead. I was going to offer you the job, and you can choose who will go with you." I nod and watch as Mitchell takes down the tents. "So, I won't have a bag on me?" My dad nods. "If Aszy is not going to carry a bag, can I ride on his back?" Lilly asks with a hopeful look. "Sorry, Lil, I'm scouting so I can't have you on my back." Lilly nods with tears in her eyes. She walks away toward our mom. I turn to my dad, "I'll have John come with me." Dad looks shocked but nods anyway. "That's a little surprising, but I'll let him know." With that, he walks off. Soon everything was ready and breakfast was done.

We ate more soup and bread. After breakfast, all of the adults shift, and the kids help to get them ready. Some of the wolves stay in their human form to help the children put the bags on the wolves while the children buckle them. Some of the bags have the carts attached to them. Many of the women had the carts. The bag I had was now on my father's back. Meanwhile, Mitch is cleaning up the camp. Jack is in his human form and is tying the tents to the bags as soon as Mitchell is done with one. John walks up to me; we nod at each other and head out. "All clear," I mind-link to the pack. Everyone starts to follow behind us as we begin scouting ahead. We are so far up that we couldn't see the others but know that they will follow our scent.

BLOODSTONE PACK

It's been a whole week, and we have lost ten female wolves to the packs we passed and gained two new ones. The twins Damick and Ray are around twenty years old and are the sons of the beta of their pack.

Lilly has bagged to ride on my back for the past week. I finally give in so she comes scouting with me. Right now, she's asleep on my back. "We should be nearing the Bloodstone pack," my father mind-links to everyone. I continue to walk, lost in thought. I'm brought out of my thoughts by the Bloodstone Pack scent.

I howl out to tell both packs that we've arrived. Mitch jumps in joy and rolls his tongue out like a dog. Lilly wakes up to my howl. "Aszy, why did you howl?" Lilly asks as she rubs her eyes. "We've arrived at the Bloodstone Pack, so I howled to let our pack know and to let the Bloodstone pack know so that they will welcome us." I answer her through the mind-link, and she nods. I soon see my father and mother and then the rest of the pack. Mom comes to me; her small brown wolf form puts her two forelegs on my back to lick Lilly's face.

"Ew! Mommy, that is gross!" Lilly laughs as she tries to half-heartedly push mom away. "Mommy, why is Aszy bigger than you and have different fur than you and Daddy?" Lilly asks our mom. I'm a jet-black wolf with royal blue eyes, while my dad is a gray wolf with golden eyes and is the same height as me, and mom is a smaller brown wolf with green eyes. She's bigger than the other wolves. She's the size of a beta. "Well, I'm the daughter of a beta, but I'm not sure about the fur," Mom answers in the family mind-link.

We reserved a howl of welcome to enter the pack. Mom removes her paws from my back, and we walk into the pack. We are greeted by four wolves. They nod to us and turn to lead us to the pack house. We soon arrive at the house. "Good afternoon, Firestorm Pack. We've been waiting for you. Your rooms are ready for you. My beta, Jackson, will show you to your room. May I speak with you, Alpha Johnson?" My father nods and follows the Bloodstone Alpha.

"Firestorm Pack, please shift and follow me." We all shift in human form. I shift once my sister gets off my back. "Aszy, can you carry me?" Lilly asks with her big brown puppy eyes. I growl in frustration as I try to not give in to her. "Come on, you know that we couldn't say no before, so why would we now?" Claude asks. If I didn't see how bloodthirsty he could be, I would say that he is the most soft-hearted wolf ever. "I'm only like that to pups and to my mate. No one else." I roll my eyes and pick up my five-year-old sister.

"Hey, 'Land you should come with me to talk to all the unmated females. One might be your mate." Mitch invites me to go with him, and the hope of my mate being here makes me want to go. I'm about to say sure when Claude speaks up. "Our mate is not here," he tells me. "How do you know?" I ask. Claude huffs and stays quiet. Fine, whatever. "Sorry Mitch, but I'm going to help my dad out." I turn and follow Beta Jackson. After a while, Jackson comes to a black door. "This will be your room, Alpha Asland Johnson." I nod and walk into the room that I will stay in for the night. "Where's my room?" Lilly asks sweetly as she hugs my left leg, stopping me from walking any farther. "You, little one, are staying with your mother and father in their room here," Beta Jackson says, pointing to the door across the hall. Just then, mom walks out of the room. "Mommy!" Lilly lets go of my leg and runs to our mom.

I walk into the room and drop onto the bed. I'm startled awake by my door bursting open. "I found her!" John, my other best friend, yells. "Congrats man. Now get out before I kill you for waking me up." I'm really happy for John, but I hate being woken up. "Oh no, John, you woke up the sleeping beauty," Mitchell says in mock fear. They both start laughing.

I growl loudly, "That's it, you're both dead!" I jump out of the bed and chase them. As soon as we were all outside, we shifted into wolves. We tackled each other. Mitchell was a dark brown and red wolf, and he is a bit smaller than me. John is the same size or maybe a little smaller then Mitchell, and he is a blonde wolf with a little bit of brown mixed in. John is my top warrior wolf, while Mitchell is my beta. They try to pin me down together but me being an Alpha made it really hard. "I'm not going down easily," I mind-link them as they run at me. I pinned Mitchell under me while I got John by the neck.

"We give," they both mind-link me, and I'm about to let go of John's neck when a blood curling scream is let out. John instantly tenses up. I feel someone ram into me with all their strength, though there isn't enough to affect an alpha. Even if I'm not a full alpha, my strength is on par with one. I let go of John so he doesn't get hurt by my teeth. I turn and see a very small whitish-gray wolf. I sniff the air and smell a she-wolf. My eyes widen as she growls at me and stands in front of John. "Let me guess, she's your mate," I mind-link John. He gives a wolfish smile and nods. I turn back to the still growling little she-wolf. Surprisingly, my spirit wolf is calm about this. "That's because she's an omega, and it's cute that she thinks she can fight me" says Claude. I mentally roll my eyes. I shift and look at the small she-wolf.

Omegas are the size of normal wolves. "It's okay. I wasn't really going to kill John. Please shift so we can talk," I request. The she-wolf shifts, "Sorry Alpha, I just saw what was happening and panicked." I cut her off with a shake of my head. "It's fine. John is one of my best friends, and we fight a lot so you'll see this quite often. Just know that I'll never purposely hurt him. Well, not too badly," I add when John whispers something about never living up to my threats. He freezes, and the girl nods with a smile. "Oh, I didn't get your name."

She smiles and says, "Jillyn, but you can call me Jill." I nod and hold out my hand. She hesitantly shakes it. "Nice to meet you, and welcome to our pack." She smiles and runs into John's arms. "Boys, dinner is ready." We head to the kitchen. After dinner, I go back to my room and take a nice long shower. "Dude, you sound like a she-wolf," Claude says. Can you blame me? I haven't showered in a week." I get changed and go to bed.

ROGUES

I wake up and force myself out of the comfortable bed. I grab a blue t-shirt and jeans to change into. I leave the room with a small bag of clothes on my back and then enter my parents' room. "Oh, good morning, Bear." I smile at mom and put my small bag of clothes into the family bag. "Morning. I'm going out running," I tell her as I feel my restless spirit wolf. "Okay, just make sure the Bloodstone Alpha knows." I nod and look for the alpha or a pack member. I soon see a Bloodstone pack member. "Excuse me, could you ask your alpha if I can go on a quick run before heading out?" The man nods and blanks out. "What's your name?" After saying my name, he blanks out and returns. "Alpha says you can. Also, he says that your father wants to see you after your run." I thank him and run to the woods.

I let Claude take control and shift. After about ten minutes Claude gives me back control. I shift and walk back to the pack house. "Son, I need to talk to you." I nod as I follow him to the alpha's office. We enter the office. "What did you want to talk about?" I notice that the Bloodstone Alpha and Luna are in the room along with my mom. Okay, something is up. "I agree that this is not normal for just talking to your son," Claude says and goes on high alert. I put on a calm front as I nod to the Bloodstone leaders.

"Please sit." The Bloodstone Alpha says as he gestures to the chairs. I sit down and look at my father, confused. "Asland, I know this must be confusing, but since you will be the next alpha your father thought it best for you to be a part of this meeting." I look at the Bloodstone Alpha when he addresses me. "And what is this said meeting?" I ask respectfully to the other alpha. "It's a meeting about the rogues of this area," my father answers. "Rogues! Of course it had to be about those filthy mutts," Claude growls in annoyance.

"What about them?" I ask, trying to keep Claude's annoyance out of my voice. "Well, they are a bit active around as of late. They are also coming in more numbers, which we all know is strange itself, and them with an attack pattern, it is way too strange." This catches Claude's attention. "An attack pattern?" I echo his question out to the others. "Yes, for the past year they've attacked like they are looking for something or someone." I wonder what it could mean? "Maybe someone has taken control of the rogues," Claude growls and then suddenly stops. "Let me have control?" Claude pleads with me. I quickly let go of control. Claude has never asked for control before.

"Father, can you get me a map of the ten territories?" My father nods, knowing my wolf is in control. "Claude, what's the matter?" Mom asks, fear clearly in her voice. The Bloodstone Alpha looks confused. Dad runs back into the office with a large map. "Mother, can you get me a red and a black marker?" She nods and goes to get them as Claude unfolds the map. "What's wrong?" I ask, because someone decided to block their mind. "Asland, something is very strange about the rogues," observes Claude.

Claude starts to circle all of the territories in black and puts a red X where the rouges attacked. How he knows that information is beyond me. Once he's done, he turns to my parents and the Bloodstone leaders. "The rogues attacked all of these territories, but out of ten territories, only ours was burned." Everyone's eyes widen. The Bloodstone Alpha looks at his computer and types something. "That's true; only the Firestorm Pack's house was burned down."

"Rogues don't normally burn pack houses. Someone must have control over them," Claude growls as he paces around. "But who would it be?" The Bloodstone Luna asks no one in particular. "Could they be looking for the boy?" Everyone turns and looks at my dad. "What boy?" the Bloodstone Alpha asks. "Well, my pack has carried this old prophecy about a boy born of the wolf, who will rise with fire and unite two species or something like that." A boy wolf born will rise with fire and unite two species?

"It's us," Claude tells me. "What do you mean?" I ask him. "We are the boy of the prophecy," he says. "You don't know that. There are a lot of boys who are born of the wolf," I tell him. "Yes, but can they run through a burning building and not get a single burn?" Claude points out and then he gives me back control.

"I'm the boy in the prophecy," I announce. Everyone looks at me. "And why would that be, son?" asks my dad. I look at him and say, "In the fire, I wasn't burnt whatsoever." This got the Bloodstone Alpha's attention. "You were in a fire and didn't get burned?" he asks me. I nod and wonder what this could mean for me? "Wait, if they are looking for the boy, wouldn't they already know it's me when I came out of the house?" Everyone gets lost in their thoughts. "I'm not sure, we did chase them away before you jumped out of the window."

"How would the rogues even know about this prophecy? This is our first time hearing about this." the Bloodstone Luna says. Dad sighs, "This proves that my older brother is in the center of this mess. He will be the only one who has this knowledge. Though, why attack so many territories but only burn ours? Especially since he wants it for himself," Dad growls at the end. "Maybe he wasn't looking for the boy, but testing his hold over the rogues before attacking you. They could have attacked you to get you off guard and then returned to finish you off. You can always rebuild the pack house," The Bloodstone Alpha comments as he rubs his beard.

"We need to get to the pack house soon," Claude says with something in his voice that I can't put my finger on. "What's the hurry? If the rogues are after me, wouldn't it be safer here?" I ask Claude. "No, we need to get to the pack house," he says and I feel him getting restless. "Dad, we need to get to the pack house faster. The sooner we get there, the sooner we can set up protocols," I tell him. Dad looks at the map. "If we run in wolf form without the carts, we will be able to get there in a week instead of two, but that will put the children in danger," he announces.

I'm not going to put the pack in danger. "Asland, only we need to get there. The pack can take their time. Something is calling me and telling me to hurry," Claude says, sounding very confused and restless. "Claude wants to get there fast but not at the risk of the pack. We will go ourselves and then you and the pack can get there in two weeks." I see my mom shaking her head. "No, you can't go by yourself," she tells me. I give her a warm smile. "I'll take Mitch, John, and his mate with me." I notice mom relaxing a little. "Is that okay dad?" He nods and I leave the office.

I walk around, looking for my two best friends. I could just mind-link them, but this is something I want to say in person. I soon find them in the game room with the other teens in our pack and the teens in the BloodStone pack. "Mitchell and John, I'd like a word with you." They both instantly became serious and stoned-faced at my tone. They follow me out of the game room and into the room I was given.

"What is it?" Mitchell asks, all his playfulness gone. "I was wondering if you two will go with me to the pack house. My wolf is telling me that I must go to the pack house quickly. Will you two come with me?" They straighten up and, in unison, say, "Yes, Alpha." I ttell them we will leave after breakfast. They turn to leave and get their stuff ready. "Oh, and Jill is coming as well." This brings a huge smile on John's face. I walk to my parent's room and grab the small bag of my clothes. I swing it over my shoulder and head for the kitchen. Mitch, John, and Jill enter the room after me. We all eat and then say our goodbyes.

I shift and grab the small bag strap between my teeth. Mom walks up to me and hugs my neck. "Please stay safe, Asland." I nod as she hesitantly lets go of me. "Let's go." I mind-link Mitchell and John. I don't have a link to Jill but John does so it'll be okay. "Yes, Alpha," they reply. I start walking, warming up my muscles before running. The others follow my lead. After ten minutes, I start to run. I have to keep in mind that we have an omega among us, but surprisingly, she keeps up very well. Okay, new pack land, here we come.

New Home

For a whole week we ran, hunted, and slept. My legs are so tired and my paws are sore. I'm sure that the others are the same, if not worse. Right now, I'm walking around, looking for a place to sleep while the other three are resting. I look up at the sky. The sun is setting very low. I should get back. I'm about to turn back when something catches my eye. The pack house. It's the pack house! I let out a joyful howl. "Guys, I found the pack house," I mind-link the other three. I instantly hear three howls joining mine. I run to the house, and once I am at the front door, I shift. I walk up to the door and look for the lock pad. Once I find it, I put the code in, unlocking the door. I enter the dark house, lit only by the light of the setting sun through the windows.

I walk through the empty halls and stairs up to the alpha's floor. Which is on the tenth floor. Yes! We have elevators but right now everything except the safety system is turned off. I get to the tenth floor and am greeted by a small hallway with only one door with a sign. I'm shocked by what the sign says. "Alpha Asland Johnson," what does this mean? I slowly open the door to an office. It is a bit dark, but the fading light from the window is enough to see the key things in the room. The room is spacious with a desk and a door to the right, and there is another door on the far wall next to the elevators, three chairs, a couch, and a bookshelf. I walk to the door farthest from the desk. It is way too dark to see anything in it. I close the door and walk to the door near the desk. I open the door and am greeted by hallways and more doors. I walk in the first door to my right. It is hard to see in it with the sun setting.

It is a very small room. I barely even fit inside it. I feel around and find a box-like thing on the wall. I feel it is a flat surface, but right when my hand touches the surface, the screen lights up. This must be the activation system. I put in the six-digit password my dad gave me for the activation system. "Man, it's dark in here. Where are the lights?" Mitchell mind-links me, no longer sounding dead tired.

I look at the screen and see a list of everything. I slide through the list until I see electricity. I click on it and screen changes to a list of everything that needs electricity with red dots off to the side. I scroll down and see an "activate all" electricity button on the bottom of the page. I slide it on and, instantly, the red dots become green. I hve to close my eyes as the room bursts with lights. Okay, the electricity is on. I go back to the home page. I scroll through the list. I turned on the alarm systems, water, air conditioning, and everything else that I can turn on. I left the furnace off since it is summer. I walk out of the small room. I walk through the hallway, opening all the doors. I find a kitchen, a gym, six bathrooms, four bedrooms, ten closets, two patios, and a greenhouse. Each room has a bathroom and closet but nothing else. Only one room has a bed in it.

I walk back to the bedroom that has the bed in it. I climb in and let the darkness take me. I wake up to the sun in my eyes. I don't want to get out of bed. I groan into the pillows. "We need to mark the territory," Claude growls at my laziness. I sigh and drag my body away from the bed. I walk to the end of the hall to the office. I walk to the desk and see the area mapped out. The territory is huge. It's going to take me all day to mark all of this.

"THERE IS NO FOOD!" I hear Mitchell yell from who knows where. At least it isn't through the mind-link. "Dude, what did you expect? Everything was turned off." I mind-link him. "But food," Mitchell whimpers through the link. "You're pathetic," I tease back then open the link between John and Mitchell, only to discover another one. I try to open it but it stays closed. Why is it there and who is it?

I know it is not Jill's, since she has not gone through the pack ritual. I decide to put it to the back of my mind and open John's and Mitchell's links. "John, Mitch, go and hunt. John, tell Jill to gather berries and herbs. I'm going to mark the territory so I'll be gone all day." I look around and notice a private elevator. Awesome! I walk to it and click the arrow button. The doors instantly open. I walk in and click the first floor button. The doors slide shut, and I glance around. It is pretty spacious; it could probably fit about ten people in it and still have comfortable space between them.

Soon, the doors open. I walk out and see another elevator next to it, but this one is black. On the black elevator door is a sign, "Alpha Asland Johnson". I walk into the other elevator and see only nine floors. I exit and walk back to my elevator. Instead of an arrow button, there's a hand scanning pad. "Asland, you saw the two elevators. Can we go marking now?" Claude is very restless, and I wonder why.

"If I knew the reason, I would have told you by now." I shrug and walk to the front door. Then, I walk out of the house. I'm instantly greeted by the warmth of the summer heat. I run and jump off the stairs. I shift in midair, landing on my front paws. Claude claws to the surface of my mind. I let go of control of my body. Claude instantly takes over and heads west. After running for about two hours, we find the pack marker. He scratches the trees near it then rubs a permanent scent into the fresh scratches. Finally, at the last marker, Claude grabs it between his teeth and yanks it out of the ground. Claude throws the last marker far out of the territory. With the sound of the metal hitting a rock or something similar, Claude let's out a fearsome howl for those who might be a threat to his new pack. I've never heard this howl, so raw with power that I did not know we had in us.

ALPHA

For the past week, John, Mitchell, and me take turns patrolling the territory. John and Mitchell patrol together at different sides of the territory. I take the night patrol. Jill has become an amazing cook over the past week. I can't wait for my family and pack to arrive so we can set up regular patrolling shifts. A howl breaks me out of my thoughts.

"They're here!" Jill yells repeatedly as she runs around the pack house. I leave the game room and go to greet my family and friends. Once outside, I shift and run to the border of the territory. Mitchell and John soon flack behind me. I let out a joyful howl as I see my father. I shift back into a human. Mom pulls me into a tight hug. I return it immediately. Dad clears his throat to get our attention. I turn to him, only to get attacked with a hug by Lilly. I pick her up and look at my dad to see what he wanted to say. "Yes, dad?" He smiles, "so do you like your birthday present?"

I look at him, confused about what he means. "What presents?" Dad points toward the house. "The pack house was meant to be your eighteenth birthday present, with or without a mate," he says. I'm shocked at this statement. No wonder he allowed me to choose the new pack location without question. I remember that day like it was yesterday. "I agree, I remember that we felt drawn to this place," Claude says, popping up for the first time since finishing the marking.

My father announces, "Now that you know this, I'm stepping down. I, Alpha Jersëy Johnson, step down from being the Firestorm Pack's alpha and entrust it to my son Alpha Asland Mark Johnson with his beta, Mitchell Joe Dailyn, his delta, John Florlyn, and his delta female, Jill Flower Florlyn." Instantly, power surges through me. I also notice that Mitchell and John stand straighter, and Jill blushes like crazy. It's not uncommon to instantly putt the last name of the male wolves to the she wolves, even if they are not yet married. Wolves have a marriage ceremony with the absolute certainty that we have an eternal marriage.

I smile and turn to Jill. "Jill Flower Florlyn, do you promise to protect and provide for the Firestorm pack?" Jill smiles, "I do." Her voice is strong and holds no hesitation. The omega of the past is no longer there. All that is there is a strong delta female that I am glad to welcome into my family. I return her smile and ask, "Do you promise to be truthful to your fellow pack mates and to not betray pack secrets to another pack?" She nods, "I do."

I grab the golden knife that a pack member holds out. I slice it down my palm. The pack member takes the knife and cleans the blood off before handing it to Jill. Jill slices her palm and we shake hands. Our blood mixes together, forming the pack connection. Instantly, I feel a new thought in my head. I open the link. "Welcome to the pack," I tell her. She smiles and replies out loud, "I am proud to be the new delta female." Cheers irrupt through the crowds.

I do this with three other girls. Dad clears his throat, getting everyone's attention. "It is now time for the new alpha and beta to go on their first run as alpha and beta." Mitchell steps out of the crowd. He nods to me and shifts. His dark brown and red wolf shakes his fur. I shift into my wolf and walk up to my beta. "Dude, you're even bigger than before," Mitchell says on the pack link. Everyone laughs. "That's because he now has all the alpha power," my dad explains.

I nod to Mitchell. I let out a howl, and the rest of the pack joins in. After the howl, I race into the woods. Mitchell runs right behind me. "I can't believe that I'm a beta now," Mitchell says in our private link. "Mitch, you were always a beta, you just have the title now," I tell him. Mitchell laughs as we continue our run. "Now, all we need to find are the luna and beta females." I nod, "Yes. I wonder which one comes first." We both laugh.

"Wow, we already made it to the end of the territory," Mitchell says as we look over the cliff. The run takes us so long that the sun is starting to set. I lay down with my forepaws over the edge of the cliff. Mitchell's reddish black wolf lays next to me. I close my eyes and focus on the pack bond. In my mind, the pack link is a large gold ball of light. It's surrounded by many smaller ones. The small ones are all different colors and sizes. Some are connected to each other, and all of them are connected to the gold ball. I focus on my mom. Soon, a bright light pink ball appears connected to two other balls. The green one is my father, while the yellow one is my sister. I gently grab onto my mom's ball. It's warm to the touch. I smile as I feel her send her joy and pride through the bond. I let go and focus. It's a lot easier to focus on the bond now. "That's because we are now the alpha and everyone is connected to u,." Claude says the pride is so clear in his voice. We lay there in silence as the sun sets. "Come on, Mitch," I mind link him as I get up. He quickly follows suit. I howl as I run. Mitchell joins, and soon I hear all of the pack howling as we run back to the house to begin our new roles in life.

Unbridled Sorrow

I open my eyes as the alarm goes off. I sigh as I climb out of bed. I take a quick shower and get ready for the day. I pick up my phone to see what is on my schedule for today. I've been the alpha for a year now. I've yet to find my mate or even find a clue of her presence. Claude is going mad at the thought of not finding her soon. Almia is getting even more annoying than ever. She refuses to back off, though Claude has come very close to killing her on multiple occasions. I walk into my office and see my dad there at my desk. He looks up and smiles, "Hey, son. I thought I'd help today so you can have a break. I know I really enjoyed it when my father did that for me." I sit down on the couch, I look out the window just as John runs out chasing his three-year nephew. Jill standing in the doorway holding their new pup. I wish I had my mate to please and care for like they do- to honor and protect. I sigh and turn to dad. His smile has become even more gentle.

"Don't worry son, she will come." I nod as I lean against the couch. "When did you meet mom?" I ask as I stare at the ceiling. "I met her when I was seventeen and at a human school no less. I smelled her around the school. At first, I just thought it was a new scent that one of the human girls sprayed." I grimace at the remembrance of the perfume the high school girls always sprayed in the halls; at least they didn't try to bathe in it. Dad laughs, "I know exactly what you are thinking, oh boy, were those times the worst. Well, anyway, I followed the scent and was so focused on finding the source of it that I almost ran into a tree." I laugh at this and Dad joins in, thenhe continues after we are done laughing. "I was so confused as to why the tree smelled so good. I was just about turn back when someone jumped onto my back. I completely go wolf on them, and then it turned out to be your mom."

I laugh at the thought of Mom on Dad's back as he wolfs out. "How far did you shift?" I ask. Unlike our pack mates, alphas have the ability to shift any part of our body. When mourning the loss of another member, pack members are half wolf and half human. This is basically like a wolf standing up, but you can't communicate in this form, so only the mind-link works during this time, just like when in full wolf form. Normally, you are in that form for as many days as the years the person who has passed has been alive. An alpha mourns with the other pack members and often stays in that form for a longer period of time than the others. I have been in this form three times in my life, although I haven't yet experienced it as an alpha.

"Oh, only my nails became claws and my fangs came out," Dad answers, breaking me out of my thoughts. "Oh, okay," I close my eyes and, instantly, the pack bond is there. I've been working on strengthening the bonds with my pack mates, since I get much stronger from the bonds. It goes both ways; they also get stronger when this happens. I pour some of my power through the bonds. "It still surprises me that you already know how to do that at such a young age. I can also feel how strong the bond is now. In fact, I think that you have a stronger bond with the pack than even I did. That's all well and dandy but son, be careful. For as strong as these bonds are, if a member passes, the pain will be excruciating." His voice speaks volumes, and I open my eyes to see worry filling his eyes.

I walk over to console him, and instantly start to feel like I got shot in the heart multiple times. I fall to my knees as tears fill my eyes. Someone has died, but who? I close my eyes and call forth the pack bond. It is one of the new wolves. One that just learned to shift. Another ball of light disappears. I cry out in pain. I faintly feel arms around me and someone calling out to me. I open my eyes as the third one disappears. "We are under attack," I whisper through the pain. Dad howls out a warning to the pack. Claude sends me strength as I stand up and walk, though I almost fall over with each death. There are so many in such a short time. Claude howls in pain and anger. He claws to get out and fight. I run down the stairs, my panic making me run faster than ever before. I get to the third floor, and I burst through the window and shift into a wolf. For a split second, I want to laugh. What's with me and the third story windows? I land, shake out the tension in my shoulders, and run to find the rogues. Five rogues appear in front of me. I growl as I lift my head up high. I force myself not to curl up into a ball because of the pain. I go for the attack, but another member dies, which throws me off balance. I fight through the pain and go back to the battle. One of the rogues gets a good attack on my right foreleg. I growl and yank him off of me.

I continue to fight through the rogues that seem to be never-ending. Every time I take one down, two take his place. My legs give out from under me as I feel six of my pack member's bonds disappear. With Claude's help, I force myself to stand up. I can already feel my power as an alpha fading, though it will never truly disappear even if everyone else disappears since I was born an alpha. Though I'd either die than be the only survivor of my pack. I fade into the distance as Claude takes over to fight. I look at the pack bond, so many balls of light are gone. My heart shatters as I start to see the pups' lights disappear. They've gotten into the safe house and are killing the pups. I scream as the pain fills my very soul. Dad was right- the pain of each death is excruciating. I pull the pack bond into my arms and hold onto each one, pouring my power into them, hoping that will be enough to save them. My soul shatters as I feel my sister's bond disappear. I howl in pure anguish, and I feel Claude howl as we both lose the will to fight. I feel them put something over my neck, but I don't care anymore. I feel a tug on my neck, and after three more tugs, I get up and follow. I soon feel something cold on my paws. I hear metal clicking together. I don't care about my outer surroundings as I cry, holding onto the golden ball of the pack bond that is fading away. Everyone has died, and I am all alone.

Something's Wrong

"Jaylen, please focus on the meeting." I turn at my mother's voice. I do find these meetings a little redundant since it usually just repeats old information. Even so, I normally don't space out. I just feel like something bad is going to happen. "I'm sorry, mother. I feel a little off today. May I please be excused for today?" I ask softly, as she looks at me with worry. "All right, dear." A guard pulls out my chair. I give my mother and father a curtsy and turn away. I get ten steps in when I'm suddenly hit with such anguish and pain that I fall to my knees, screaming. I hear chairs falling and feet running, but they are all in the distance. "Jaylen this isn't our pain!" Ruby, my phoenix, says in a panic. "I know, we need to find him, NOW!" I shout within myself, just as I feel the anklet on my right ankle heat up. Soon, I burst into flames. My body burns into ashes; instantly, the ashes start forming into my phoenix self. I let out a call, sending a burst of fire magic out of my wings. My golden feathers are in their fire stage. I launch myself into the air and take off toward the place my mate was born.

I soon see scorched earth. I dive down toward the land. As I get closer, I open my wings, and the air slams into me. I drift down and land on the burnt ground. I look around. Many of the trees are burnt and so are the buildings around one of the bigger pack houses. I walk toward the building in the center. Since my mate is a child of the alpha, he would mainly be in the pack house. I look at the building, a majority of it is still standing. I gently walk onto the building, the floorboards creak with my weight. I walk to the center of the room. I turn to the sky and call forth the memories within the ashes. Soon, I'm flooded with many black and white scenes that this home has seen- so many generations of alphas and their families. I focus and call forth the most recent ones. I know this fire isn't what caused my mate so much anguish. It happened a year ago, so not recently. I soon see a gorgeous man running through the fire in a panic, jumping and dodging fallen objects. I watch as he runs down the flight of stairs two at a time. The clothes he's wearing are on fire, but this does not worry me. I know instinctively that this is my mate.

Soon, he jumps out of the window of the third floor. He rolls to get the flames off. Someone drops a fire blanket over him. I lose sight of him as he gets surrounded by his worried pack members. After a while, I see him again talking to an older male. Soon, the older male calls out to the pack. The pack gathers their family, and a few of the members shift into their wolf form, and then all of them head into the forest toward the direction from where I came. I drop the connection and shake off the memories of centuries. I turn to the direction of my home. I flip my wings as I peer into the forest. I launch myself into the air yet again, though this time I stay low as I search for signs of my mate.

I shake my head; of course, there won't be signs here. It's been over a year since he's been here. I land on a large tree that will be strong enough to hold me. "Ruby, can you use your link to help the search"' I ask my phoenix hoping that the mark she put on him at birth will help. "I feel the link, though it's very weak," she replies. Hope rises in my heart at her words. "Jaylen, I want to find him just as much as you do, but this isn't going to work." Ruby says softly, almost as if she didn't want to say it at all.

I inwardly sigh as I ruffle my feathers. I open my wings and take off once more toward home, although I'm not really going home. Soon, the mountain that contains my clan comes into sight. I land onto another tree near a cliff. "Oh, my dear brother. Oh how the mighty have fallen," a deep male voice says, and a deep growl follows suit. I tilt my head to the right toward the voices. I see a man standing over another who is bound and has a collar on his neck. "What have you done?" I can clearly hear the venom in the collared man's tone. The man without a collar laughs, "this little thing?" the man asks as he yanks on what appears to be a leash. "This breaks the bonds of a pack. To an alpha, it'll be as if they had died." The collared man's eyes widen in horror. "What have you done to my son?!" the collared man growls out, full of fire and venom. "I haven't done anything to my nephew, yet," the man says with just as much venom. I try to get a better view only to break a branch with my head. I instinctively dissolve my flames, dimming my inner light. The man swirls around, searching for the source of the noise. The man punches the one in the collar and walks away. I stay still for a long time, until I am certain that he is gone.

I shift and climb down the tree, careful not to make a sound. I hiss as I step onto a sharp rock. I wish I still had my shoes on when I shift, but, sadly, my clothes are the only thing that stay on me. Well, they are actually my feathers in the form of clothes. The man in the collar turns to me and glares. I put a finger to my lips and look around. I see no one and turn back toward the man. He is still glaring at me. I slowly walk toward him with my arms out as though he is a frightened animal, which he basically is at this point. Once I'm close enough to him to hear his breathing, I stop. My eyes widen as an old but very familiar scent hits me. "It's our mate's scent. This man is somehow related to our mate," Ruby says, confirming my suspicions. I take a deep breath and relax at the scent of my mate. The collared man lets out a growl, "Who are you?!" I instantly cover his mouth with my hands. "Quiet, we don't want that evil man to come back," I whisper as I search the area. He throws his head to the side, making my hands leave his face. His dark green eyes bore into mine. "Answer me?" he asks in a whisper that is still full of venom.

"My name is Jaylen, and I'm looking for my mate. In fact, you have his scent on you." I answer his question softly as if speaking to a deer. The collared man's eyes widen, "your mate." He sniffs the air, "You aren't a wolf and are definitely not human. What are you?" I'm about to answer when I hear someone coming. I run to a tree and climb it. It's the evil man; he pauses and sniffs around. "What do you want, Kelob?" the collared man growls out the name. Kelob kneels on one knee. "I want you to submit to me. Only an alpha can take these off. Even then, I'll make sure your wolf never rears its ugly head. Although the longer you have this collar on, the more damaged your bond with your wolf becomes." The collared man growls deeply, yet you can hear his exhaustion. Kelob pushes a button on a black box. "Now, now, it seems you forgot how to treat your alpha." The man screams and his body converses.

I feel sorry for the man and some anger as well. "That's because he is our mate's father." My eyes widen at Ruby's words. "Now, if none of the older wolves submit to me, I'll kill all of them for real and take the pups." My mate's father tries to attack the man, only to get shocked again.

I can feel my inner flames roaring to get out. "Now Jersëy, submit to me, and I'll free you." My mate's father, who I now know as Jersëy, growls. Kelob growls back as he pushes the button. He turns and walks away. I wait for a long period of time before going to Jersëy again. "Are you alright?" I ask, hoping he hears my sincerity. He glares at me, but I notice it's softer now. "Do you know where the other members of your pack are?" I asking, trying to figure out how to help. He shakes his head. "I know that they are alive based on Kelob's taunts, alhough they are separated all over the territory. These collars seem to cancel out our wolves, which makes it so we can neither sense each other nor can we communicate." He answers, his voice very weak from all the screaming. I've read a lot about werewolves; they share a deep connection with each other, especially with their wolf counterparts. Wait, they share their strength though their bond, so if I can substitute that bond temporarily, that might work! "Jersëy, I have an idea. I think I will be able to give everyone a temporary bond that will help gather your strength." Jersëy's eyes widen and he asks, "How?"

I smile and pull out one of my golden feathers on my right arm. I hiss at the pain, but it quickly heals. I hand him the feather. In my human form, the feather is about a foot long, though in my bird form, it is so much bigger. He looks at the feather in confusion, "How is this feather from your costume going to do to help my pack?" He says, starting to get angry. I sign and focus on my dismembered feather. Instantly, it lights up with its beautiful golden flame- the flame of death. This will be the last time it lights up. Of course, the ashes will come back to me and form a new feather. Jersëy freaks out and quickly throws the feather away from him. The feather drifts slowly to the grass, though the flames stay only on the feather. Jersëy stares at it in complete wonder. "Do not worry, the flame will not harm you." I smile at him gently, and he takes a deep breath and picks up the flaming feather. "How did you do that?" he asks as he stares at the feather, turning it and watching as the fire moves around the feather to be upright yet never straying from it. "This is how you will be able to share your strength and give it to your son. The more you put into the feather, the larger and brighter the flame will be. The power will go to my other feathers. If I give everyone in your pack a feather and they give it their hope and love, that strength will come to me." He looks at me in suspicion. I smile and say my final line, "Then, I will be able to transfer that to my mate."

He raises his eyebrow, "And why would we want to give your mate the last of our strength?" he asks. I smile gently at him. It's a fair question, and it's not like he knows that it's his son. "That's because your son is my mate." His eyes widen and then he laughs, really laughs, full of joy and not bitterness. "Oh, my son would kill me if he knew that I met his mate before him. I don't know how, but I know that you are telling me the truth." He smiles at me for the first time and then looks back at the feather. "How are you going to find him?" he asks, his voice deep with worry for his son and family.

"If he is touching fire, then I am able to sense him." He looks at me in concern, "You want my son to be on fire?" he asks, more in confusion than in anger. "Yes, since my power stops the flames from hurting him, that will be how I will be able to sense him." He nods and turns to the feather which is now just a flicker. He focuses on the feather which soon bursts anew. A flame, small but bright. "Please, help my son and save my family." I know that his family isn't just his mate and children, he means his entire pack. "Of course," I say with a courtesy. He looks at me, confused. "Sorry, I do that out of habit and my upbringing."

I turn and run into the forest. I ignore the pain in my feet as I run. I give feathers and instructions to those I pass. Many, if not all of them, are very suspicious of me. After telling them about Jersey, though, many don't believe I am their alpha's mate. They give me a fraction of their trust. I still have no clue as to the name of my mate. I lean against a tree and look at my wounded feet as they start to heal. This is the seventh time I have had to rest. I've found three people with collars, and I avoided the wolves and people without them. This would be a whole lot easier if I could be in bird form. I am able to change my size to that of a macaw, even though I will lose the ability to speak. After my feet are fully healed, I start my quest once more. I'm trying to do this as quickly as possible so as to not give the evil wolves more time to torment my mate. Soon, the sun starts to set. The darker it gets, the more my feathers will be visible. I need to go faster. I should have asked how many members are in this pack. I know a pack can range from fifty to four hundred or more members.

I find four more members with collars, so I do the usual thing and continue on my way. So far, all of them have been tied to trees or bound enough that they can barely move their hands. I trip over a root; this is definitely not the first time this happened, and I know that it will not be the last. This time I trip because of the pure panic I feel through the bond that is half complete. That awful man is doing something to my mate. I need to hurry and gather all the strength the pack has left so I may transfer it to my mate. I'm not completely sure how I'll do that.

I look up as I hear multiple screams from small children. I see around fifty to sixty children chained to each other by their collars. I smile gently to try to calm them down and slowly walk toward the children. One little girl catches my attention. She is looking at me with hope instead of fear. I walk to her and kneel down, "Hello dear. My name is Jaylen. I'm here to help you and everyone in your pack," I say. She looks to the other children then back to me. "Do you know where Papa, Mama, and Aszy are?" she asks somewhat clearly. I wish I could answer her, but so far, I have only met my mate's father.

"I'm sorry, I have met many of your pack members, although I don't know who is connected to whom." The little girl looks saddened by my words, so I tell her, "I do have a solution." I pull out another feather; many of them have grown back. "With this magic feather, you can give your family strength. Though, sadlym you are not able to speak with them." I light a tiny flame and hold it out to her. She looks at the feather with fear. "Do not be afraid. This is a magic feather. The fire will not harm you." I say, and to prove my point, I slap my hands together with the feather in between them. Of course, fire is unable to harm me in any way.

I open my palms again. The feather lays flat against my right palm, still with its tiny flame. "See, no harm done. Many of your pack have similar feathers. I will be taking all your hope and love to your alpha." Her eyes widen, "Aszy!" It takes me a moment to realize that Aszy is the alpha. "Is Aszy your alpha?" I ask, though I doubt that is his real name. She shakes her head. "Aszy is my brother, others call him Alpha." Oh, so she is my mate's little sister. "I promise to save your pack mates and your brother." I hand the other children feathers and search for more members. I run through the forest with a smile. I now have a hint to what my mate's name might be.

I hear a growl and quickly hide behind a tree. I'm about to climb it when someone speaks. "Come out right now. I know you're there, as the beta of this pack, I'll never submit to the likes of you." I walk out from behind the tree. The young man eyes widen for a brief moment before going to an icy stare. His green eyes and blonde hair stand out quite a bit. He seems so familiar, though I can't put my finger on why. Then his words "as the beta." Register. He is my mate's beta. An alpha has a very strong tie to their beta. "Perfect," he growls, and I realize I said that out loud. "Beta of the Firestorm Pack." The beta stands to attention at the title. "I'm here to save this pack." His eyes narrow in suspicion. "Why would you save this pack?" A large part of me wants to claim the pack as mine and give them the protection and love they deserve, though I'll need my mate for that.

"I will protect those my mate cares for, and I will end those who try to harm him or his loved ones." I can feel power within those words; even the beta looks conflicted. "And just why would your mate care for this pack. Is he a member? Wait, he can't be. I know everyone's mates, and you're not one of them. You're definitely not mine and or the pups. That leaves four unmated males and two females." I take a step closer, and he growls at me. I pull out a feather. I have no idea what possessed me to put it in his hair. I light it just like the others and tell him, "Just believe in your alpha. You know he is still alive. Keep fighting for him, and he will be back." I whisper in his ear and run off. I don't know why but it felt like that's what he needed. I soon hear a howl of hope and strength. The moon is rising now; I need to finish this up. I need to know how many more there are. I shift and change my size to that of a macaw, though I look nothing like one.

I take off flying up through the trees. I fly up for a bit and then look down at the forest below. I see the glow of my feathers in many places. The very large group must be the children. I see that the lights have almost formed a very large circle. Strangely, it seems as though I stayed with the circle and found the members without problem. "I believe that's because of the territory marks," Ruby says. I do remember that wolves mark their territory on trees.

Though, why would that matter to me, really? Ruby sighs, "An alpha marks at least seven areas, though by the looks of this pack, he marked fourteen. You most likely did not notice, but every place you rested and let your feet heal was a marked tree." Ruby's words surprise me, though I don't dwell on what she said, for I still need to save my mate.

Soon another howl joins in with the beta's howl. Then another and another join. At the same time, the flames on the land get brighter and brighter. I feel the power of their hope and love for each other slam into me like lightning multiple times. I feel it strike with every new howl. I fly through the tree and look for the rest of the pack. I no longer need to explain; those howls will do it for me. I easily find the rest, and then I find Jersëy once more. I land in front of him. He looks at me, confused for a moment. "Jaylen, is that you?" I nod at his words, "have you gotten what you need?" I nod again, since I'm unable to speak. "Have you located my son?" I'm about to shake my head when I feel pain shoot through my body from the area between my neck and wing. I instantly feel my flame start to devour the foreign substance, though it's not in my body. My head shoots toward the south, toward the pull of my flames at a distance. I narrow my eyes. It's time to save my mate.

UNCLE

I open my eyes and see small purple flowers in front of me. I look around. I'm in a small clearing near my pack house. Instincts tells me something is wrong. I am going to head to the pack house, only to realize that I am unable to move. I look at my feet; there are iron chains on my hands and feet. "Oh, my dear nephew is awake." I look over to my left and see a man who looks a lot like my father. A weak growl comes out, and he just laughs. "Look at this pathetic alpha without a pack." I hear laughing in the background. I try to stand strong. I also notice that Claude isn't there. "What have you done to my wolf?" I ask with a growl. My uncle laughs and taps his neck. "I put a collar on you that blocks your wolf temporarily. If you submit to me, I'll free you right now. "You killed my pack and expect me to submit. I will make sure that I see you ripped apart," I growl out, the pain and anger filling me with strength I no longer have.

"I did kill them, though that pack should have been mine from the beginning, not your father's. I was the first born!" He yells the last sentence. "You're not fit to be an alpha. Alphas are leaders and caregivers. You don't want a pack, you want minions, which you appear to have plenty." I glare up at him. He shrugs, "Well you might be right. Though I'm not bonded to them, as they have gone mad without their human side. It's different if you lose your wolf counterpart, but it won't make you as mad as when you lose your humanity." He laughs and grabs my collar. "Aw, that gives me an idea. Let's see just how long it takes for a weakened alpha to succumb to the madness." My eyes widen in horror. If he can really induce madness to my system, just how long can I fight it in my weakened state.? My uncle pulls out a small box and opens it, revealing a needle syringe with green substance. I try to back up, but the chains hold me in place.

The needle goes into my neck right where the burn mark is located. Instantly, I feel my body tremble as he pushes me down, sealing my fate. I feel my body shift into my wolf form, though I'm unable to control it. I scream as I feel my bones break. It's like the first shift all over again since I don't have Claude here. "Man, I'm sure glad the witches put a sound barrier over us and the alpha kid. It would be bad if his pack heard him or he heard his pack." I can't hear what the man says as I scream while another one of my bones breaks and reforms. I open my eyes and see my uncle crouching down and looking at me. "Is it just me or is his wolf smaller than before?" My uncle asks, looking behind him. I so badly want to lunge and bite that neck of his and devour him.

Wait, what? I agree to the biting of the neck but not with eating him. I freeze as I realize that the madness is starting to take effect. Oh, no I don't want to go down this way. I want to meet my mate, to be with my family. I want to care for my pack and raise a family with my mate. I howl to the now high moon in despair. As I feel the world around me disappear. I grab onto a chain and feel tears in my eyes, why am I still fighting? There is nothing left to fight for. My pack is dead. I'm succumbing to the madness, so what is there to fight for? I yank at the chain growling and whimpering. "Why are you still fighting?! There's nothing there!" I cry as I feel my body yank on the chain yet again. I pause as I faintly hear a very familiar howl. No, that's impossible, Mitchell was killed.

I glance at the others, and they seem to not have heard the howl. It seems like it is all in my head. Just as I'm about to lower my head, another howl sounds, and it is louder this time. I try to ignore the howls since they are just in my head. My pack is dead. Another howl, this one sounding like my mother. Tears fill my eyes; this madness is torture for me, making me hear the howls of the dead. "Crap, what are the witches doing? They need to stop those howls." My eyes widen, and I realize they can hear the howls, too. Another howl. This time I listen closely. It's my father's. I cry at the howl's meaning. "I am here." I hear each and every one of my pack howl. I go to howl back, only to see a meteor heading straight at me. The rogues bolt out of here as fast as they can, though I'm stuck here. I guess that just as I find out my pack is alive, I will die.

I feel the heat as the meteor comes closer. I'm not even sure if my strange immunity to fire is going to save me this time. Is it odd of me to think that this meteor is absolutely gorgeous? It's brilliant white with gold flames. It's so beautiful, even though a meteor is really just a rock falling from outer space. The heat is now becoming unbearable, and I can already feel my skin burning. The sweet scent of vanilla and the bitterness of smoke also oddly seem to comfort me as I know for a fact that my strange immunity to fire will not be able to save me from this. I'm definitely going to die here and become nothing but ashes. I feel the impact of an object for a split second before all the pain and misery disappear into nothing. As I let go of my life, somehow, I feel as if drifting to nowhere. Wait, if I'm dead should I really be able to think?

SONIC BOOM

I turn to my mate's father and nod my head. I go back to the direction of the other piece of my inner flame that Ruby put into our mate when he was a babe. "Is that the direction of my son?" I nod. I'm not sure what they put into my mate, but my flames have easily put a stop to it and given me his location. I fly off into the sky. For this to work, I need to be very high in the sky. I fly above the clouds to the point where it is hard to breathe. I take a deep breath. I hope this works. I have only heard of one successful attempt, though in that case, the mate was a dragon, not a wolf. I lightly flip my wing, as I hesitate. "Jaylen, this is your choice. Even though I do not like it, this may be the only way." Ruby says before disappearing. For this to work, a phoenix needs to sacrifice all of the power they have. Ruby is holding a fraction of our power so that she will be able to revive me at the last second.

I close my eyes and tuck in my wings. I feel the gravity pull toward the earth, toward my mate. I open my eyes, only to see a beautiful black wolf staring up at me with awe. I see that he is chained to the ground and unable to move. This has my flames brighten in anger. I notice that his fur is burning. No, this isn't supposed to happen. I open my wings in hopes of stopping my descent. I scream as the force snaps my wings. I start to spin out of control. I feel my back hit something. I really hope that it's a tree and not my mate. I lay on the ground on my back. I see the flames form into a large fire in the shape of a phoenix. "Jaylen!" I hear Ruby shout as she has us shift into our human form with the rebirth flames. Then, I feel my body burn in an instant and the ashes start to reform.

I feel the pain fade as my ashes finish becoming human. I open my eyes and see ashes falling like snow. Fear grips my heart at the thought that they might be my mate's. "Jaylen, think about it for a little longer," Rudy says calmly. "Wait a second. I'm alive ,which means that my mate is also alive," I realize. Just as I realize the stupidity of my panic, a man is standing over me. He is absolutely gorgeous with the moon shining off the gold feathers on his right shoulder, making his black hair glow with the help of the crown made of fire. The wind blows, revealing a white cape with gold feathers embroidered on the bottom. The inside of the cape is all gold. In fact, he is dressed in all white and gold. His jacket is all white with gold trims with only three buttons on the upper torso, leaving his abs on display, and, oh boy, what a view! I shake my head to clear my thoughts; the feathered shoulder pad attached to the cape has three gold chains- one short, thick one and two long, thin ones.

He reaches out his right hand. That's when I notice the gold embroidery of feathers on the cuffs. I smile as I grab his hand. He pulls me up easily into his arms. He doesn't let go of my hand as he wraps his left arm around my wrist. "I didn't think my mate would fall out of the sky like a meteor." My eyes widen as he whispers in my ear. His deep voice sends a chill down my spine. I pull back and grab onto his face with both hands. I stare at him in shock. He smiles at me, though that's not what surprises me. It's his eyes. They have a fire burning within them. I look at his hair. It isn't the moon making his hair shine, nor is it the crown, it is just literally glowing.

"Is there something wrong?" He asks with a look of concern. "No, I'm just a bit confused." He tilts his head slightly and still looks concerned. "You are no longer a werewolf." He shakes his head, "Of course I'm a werewolf, born and raised." I am not sure what happened, but I know for a fact that he is no longer a werewolf, at least not a normal one. "Are you able to speak to your wolf?" I ask. My mate looks stunned by my question. He closes his eyes, "I'm able to sense him there, but he is unresponsive." He looks a little bit worried, though not about me now. "Could you shift for me?" This time he smirks and backs away from me. He closes his eyes and nothing happens. He opens his eyes, and this time they are full of panic and go from their gorgeous blue color to gold. Then he bursts into fire. I panic a little, as werewolves don't use fire to shift. The fire forms a wolf, and black fur seems to sprout out and wrap around the flames like a blanket, leaving spots uncovered. The inside of the his ears and down his throat to his chest and stomach are all orange with the flames. The eyes are empty now except for the flames. He opens his mouth and sticks his tongue out to the side, which would be cute in normal circumstances, but now there are flames in his mouth. Will he be able to breathe fire?

"Do you know what happened to you?" I ask cautiously, trying not to send him into a panic. The fire wolf nods. I know that this is my mate's wolf. "When you crashed into us, we turned into ashes with you. If you hadn't revived yourself so near to us, we wouldn't have been reborn." My eyes widen at the sudden voice in my head. How is this possible when the mate bond isn't complete yet? "Your flame now lives within us, keeping us alive." My mate's wolf says, and guilt starts to eat at me. "Our lovely mate, there is no need for guilt. It's not your fault and even if it was, we would forgive you completely." My mate's wolf is trying to comfort me. "My name is Claude, and my human is Asland." I literally hit my forehead with my palm. Why didn't I ask for their names in the first place? "Wait, can you read my mind?" I ask. "Not completely, just what you are thinking about the hardest. I kept hearing my mate's wolf, so I decide to introduce us," Claude says, making it as easy to understand as possible. "Oh, I'm Jaylen. My phoenix is called Rubestia, though I just call her Ruby." I introduce myself out loud without any formal setting.

Overwhelming Joy

I feel as though I'm floating down a river with no destination in sight. No pain or sorrow, only nothingness. I'm pretty sure that I'm dead right now, though I'm not sure what there is in the afterlife. Will I meet my pack? Will I be reborn? I see a white glow in the distance that looks to be coming closer. Soon, a chain made of white fire appears and wraps round my wrist. It's surprisingly warm and comforting. The chain then yanks me away from the never-ending river toward somewhere else, but I don't know where. Suddenly, I feel pain once more, though it is quickly fading. I must have shifted back into human form, and I'm alive if I'm feeling pain. Tears fill my eyes as I feel all the pack bonds flood in. I also feel my strength restoring itself, though something seems different. I open my eyes and see gray snow. Wait, not snow but ashes. I see the trees are all bare. I feel panic seize me in a tight embrace, though I know it's not my panic. Oddly enough, I feel as though it's coming from my right.

I turn and see the most gorgeous girl ever. Golden hair and bright green eyes. She is in a gown made of feathers. Most of the gown is white, but there are gold feathers on her arms. If they were designed after a bird, the gold feathers would be the remiges that give the bird the ability to fly. The feathers are only on the dress and her forearms, leaving her upper arms and shoulders bare. She also has a tiara made of fire. As odd as a tiara may sound, it fits her very well. I know that she is my mate, though I have no clue how she got here. I take a step forward and am now leaning just barely over her. Her bright green eyes widen in surprise, though only for a moment. I see her eyes trail over me, and I stay completely still so she can take it all in. Her eyes seems to stop at my mid-section. I glance down at myself and notice that I'm not completely in my clothes and my abs are on full display. I take a deep breath and calm myself just as my mate shakes her head wildly.

I take this as a sign that she is done checking me out, at least for now. I reach out my right hand, which seems to be decorated with golden feathers. I also see golden feathers on my right shoulder in the corner of my eye. She grabs my hand, bringing my attention back to her. I easily pull her into my arms. She is very light, as though the slightest breeze can take her away. I wrap my left arm tightly around her wrist at that thought and also do not let go of her hand. I lean my head toward her shoulder and smell the smoky vanilla that seemed to comfort me as I was sure I was about to die. The smell seems to be coming off of her. I inhale deeply. This is definitely her scent. I think back to the meteor; it was unlike any meteor I've ever seen. Most meteors are white with a hue of blue. However, that one was white and gold. "I didn't think my mate would fall out of the sky like a meteor," I whisper in her ear. I smile as I see a shiver go down her spine.

After a moment, she pulls back and grabs my face. She looks surprised by something. "Is there something wrong?" I ask, worried that something is wrong. "No, I'm just a bit confused." She says, though she is definitely concerned about something. "You are no longer a werewolf," she says. I shake my head at her words, "Of course I'm a werewolf, born and raised." I am not sure what happened, but I know for a fact that I'm still a werewolf. I can feel Claude, though he has yet to respond to me. "Are you able to speak to your wolf?" I almost jump at her sudden question, especially since that is just what I am thinking about. I close my eyes to get a better sense of Claude. "I'm able to sense him there, but he is unresponsive." I open my eyes. Claude has never been this silent. He should especially howl in joy for finding our mate. "Could you shift for me?"

I smile, werewolves just so happen to love showing off. I back up so I don't accidentally harm her as I shift. I think of my wolf, his shining black coat and gold eyes. Normally I feel my body shift by now, though nothing is happening. "That's because she is right," Claude says, sounding like he just woke up. "What do you mean?" I ask him. "We died in that fire but were reborn into something very different yet the same," Claude answers and walks toward the surface. Suddenly, I feel my heart burn as though it is on fire. I want to scream in agony, but Claude takes full control and takes all of the pain, too. He explains this to our mate and introduces us. Man, I feel like an idiot, I should've done that myself. "To be fair, our mate is very gorgeous, so of course you weren't thinking." I laugh at his words, which are so true. "Wait, if you were asleep through all of that, how do you know all this?" I ask, since the collar disconnected us. "That collar did block me from contacting you and from you being able to sense the other wolves since they had the same thing happen to them. Nonetheless, I was always near you, and I saw more than you may believe. In fact, I saw our mate help our pack."

He then bursts out laughing, "I even told her phoenix spirit to put the feather into Mitch's hair and told her what to say." He sends me an image of Mitchell with a flaming feather in his hair, just behind his left ear. I burst out laughing; his face is priceless. "Oh, so if we are no longer a werewolf, what are we?" I ask so that I know what to do next. "Just a moment," he says and turns to our mate. "Asland wishes to see our new form. To do this, we must be asleep." She nods, and I feel Claude lay down and close his eyes. Instantly, everything changes, and I'm back in the spirit realm where I first saw Claude. I'm currently sitting on a border that is next to both a lake and the forest. I'm facing the water, and I look completely the same. The same dark brown hair and blue eyes, though the outfit I'm in is crazy. I also have a flaming crown that matches Jaylen's. "The meteor mainly damaged our wolf body since that is what form you were in when it happened." I turn at Claude's voice.

He walks out of the trees; he looks so different yet also the same. He looks as though someone painted flames down his throat. I see the sparks and know that the flames are real. Claude also seems to have no eyes. "Can you still see?" I ask as I wave my hand. "Yes, I can see. You will also be able to as you shift." He comes and sits next to me. He stares at the water and asks, "I don't need to tell you that swimming is no longer possible, right?" Claude says his fire eyes are flaring brighter. "Not even in human form?" Claude tilts his head leaving a trial of light. "That is possible; there are no open flames in our human form." I nod as we both stare at the water. I love to swim as a wolf but that is something I am willing to give up for my mate. "What about when winter comes?" I ask, worried that if we are attacked by rogues I won't be able to help. "We will be fine, but we should only shift if there is no other choice." I nod as the scenery goes back to black as Claude wakes up.

Meeting the Pack

I'm currently petting my mate's fur as he is asleep. The flames dim to a mere flicker. I kiss his forehead and feel him lick my cheek. I jump in surprise- he is awake. He stares at me as his flames glow as brightly as before. His tongue is very soft yet dry. I stand up and look toward the group of feathers. The pack has gathered together somewhere in the distance. "Should we go?" I look down at my mate sitting up, he is still in his fire wolf form. Ruby has studied all of the supernatural creatures here, and a fire wolf is unheard of. She is a thousand years old so she definitely had the time to find them. "Are you going in that form?" I ask. He looks down at himself and flames reappear as he shifts into a human. He is still in my colors and the fire crown. He grabs my hand. "Let's go. I'll introduce you to my pack," he says as he starts walking.

I've met most of his pack mates already. Nonetheless, I go with him to be introduced properly. I will be their luna and Asland will be Fire King of the Phoenixes. Right now, we will lead this pack until one of our children is ready to become the alpha and begin as the new Fire Queen and King of the Phoenixes. I am able to feel his excitement and pride to announce his mate so clearly, it is as though they were my own emotions. We soon arrive at the pack house. Everyone is standing there with the feathers in their hands, except the beta. He still has his feather behind his left ear as he leans against a pole. I call all the feathers back to me. They crumble into ash and float over to me. The beta winkles his noise as the ash hits him in the face as they come toward me.

I can see Asland in the corner of me eye trying not to laugh. He coughs to get everyone's attention away from the ashes to himself. "I know you guys have already met her, but even so, let me introduce my mate. Jaylen Firerose of the Phoenixes." My head swings in his direction in shock, I didn't tell him my last name or my species. "I'm guessing Claude told him our species; however, I'm the one that told him our name," Ruby says, and I can feel that she's a little upset with me.

Asland looks at me and kisses my forehead. I know for a fact that the fire tiara is flaring brighter. Everyone comes to greet me and introduce themselves. It's going to take a moment for me to remember all of their names. The little girl runs up and jumps into my arms. "Are you my sister now?" she asks with a large smile. My face burns, though we are mates, we just barely met each other. "Lilly, she is going to be your sister, just not right at this moment," Asland answers calmly. I turn to him and see his head is turned away and his ears are bright red. I smile, okay, so he isn't calm. I set Lilly down, and she runs back to her mom. Jersëy is now walking up. I put a finger to my lips and slowly creep up behind Asland. He looks up as his father approaches, but his senses are on overdrive at the moment so I doubt that he'll sense me. Soon, I'm right behind him. I get onto my tip-toes and kiss the back of his neck. He stiffens, and I see his neck turn red. Suddenly, all of my feathers stand as I feel someone staring at me with bloodlust.

I search the crowd for the culprit, only to find a girl around seventeen glaring at me. I stand my ground. I have my feathers relax as I stand up straight with confidence. I stare calmly at the girl, and her anger flares higher and she runs off. I smile and turn to my mate. I was so focused on the girl that I did not hear what my mate and his dad were talking about. I shrug and hug onto Asland's right arm and lean my head close to his shoulder. Since he is pretty tall, my head only goes to his chin. I feel my muscles relax and I start to feel very sleepy. Suddenly, the arm disappears, and I come aware of my surroundings just enough not to fall. I'm about to open my eyes when I feel an arm on my back and on the back of my knees. I'm about to panic until my fire to recognizes its other half. I curl into him and fall asleep.

I wake up to see an unfamiliar room, but I'm calm because the scent tells me that it's my mate's room. I pull off my covers and get out of bed. I stand there for a moment, waiting for the familiar knocking sound of my maids. I realize that I'm in my mate's room and my maids won't be here to assist me, not that I really need it. I walk to the mirror. My hair is a complete mess and my feathers are unkempt. I smile at myself before looking for the bathroom. There are two doors, so it's fifty-fifty on which door it is. "What's behind door number one?" I say as I turn the knob. "That'll be the hallway," I say to myself.

I close the door and walk to the next one. I open it to see the bathroom, but there is no tub. I walk in and see that there is a sink, a toilet, a cupboard with soap and shampoo for men, and a glass door on a box. I open the box and look around in it. I step inside; it's just white, smooth walls and a metal circle on the ceiling. There is also a metal handle on one of the walls. I poke the metal handle, but nothing happens. I pull it toward me, and it doesn't budge. I push it to the left, nothing happens. What on earth is this handle for? I push it to the right, I shriek in pain as water hits me from above. I dive out of the box, and I land on the floor, banging my knees but that doesn't hurt as badly as the water does. I quickly shake the water off my feathers. Soon, the door bursts open and my mate comes through in a panic. He most likely heard me and felt my pain.

"Are you okay?" he asks as he kneels next to me. My face burns in embarrassment; I point to the glass box. "What is that?" His eyebrow raises, "the shower?" he asks, the confusion very clear in his voice. I nod, now his face is bright red. He coughs, "it's to wash yourself." My eyes widen, oh, so that's what it is for." "Does water harm you?" he asks, and I shake my head. "No, I'm able to be in water," I say. I feel my face is on fire as I whisper, "I just need to take my feathers off." He tilts his head in confusion, until he realizes what I mean and his face becomes bright red. "Hmm, I, Hmm didn't know… hmm that you can do that." I burst out laughing, mostly out of pure embarrassment. I lift up my arm, it lit on fire and when the fire dissolved it left only skin. He grabs and kisses my bare arm.

Next, he kisses my forehead, "I'll go get some shampoo and body wash for you." He runs off and comes back after about three minutes. After handing me the soap, he pauses and asks, "Do you want to wear clothes or your feathers?" I think about it. I don't particularly like being without my feathers. "I would not mind having pants," I tell him. He nods and walks away. I have all of my feathers dissolve and step into the shower once more. I quickly wash my hair and body and turn off the water. I towel myself dry and summon my feathers. I walk out of the bathroom, wrapping my hair and antennas in the towel. I see some pants on the bed. I slip them on, and they are a little loose but not too bad.

PACK GAMES

As I'm talking to Dad, I feel Jaylen hug my arm and lean her head against it. It feels a little strange, but I'll get used to it fairly quickly. Soon, my arm feels even more weight and I can feel Jaylen's tiredness. I gently pull my arm free. I'm prepared to catch her; however, it seems she has become aware enough to keep herself from falling. I scoop her up into my arm. "See you later, Dad." He nods, and I walk toward the house. I get to my elevator and realize one very big problem. I need to scan my hand. "Mom, could you come over to the elevator and open it for me?" I ask via a private link. "Okay, I'll be right there," she replies back. I lean my back against the wall. Jaylen is now completely asleep, and I kiss her the top of her head. Mom arrives about four minutes later. I smile at her as she takes out her phone and takes a picture. After a few more pictures, she scans her hand, and the elevator opens. She walks in after me and clicks A for Alpha Floor.

The elevator opens onto my floor, and my mom walks out to open the door to the hallway. I follow her, careful not to bump Jaylen's legs into anything. Mom opens the door and heads toward my room. I've yet to put beds or anything else in the other room. I should do that, at least for the room that will be Jaylen's. Mom opens my door. I nod my thanks and walk in. I gently lay Jaylen down onto the bed. For the first time, I actually notice the dress isn't just made out of feathers; it's literally coming out of her skin. I'm careful not to pull or bend a feather. I gently pull the covers from under her and cover her with them. I look at the time; it's seven o'clock at night. I should do a bit of paperwork before heading to bed in one of the guest rooms on the floor below. I walk to my office and start looking over the maintenance plans and costs.

I wake up to a loud shriek and pain on my arms and back. I instantly know that the pain belongs to my mate. I bolt out of bed and run up the stairs, into my office, though the door to the hallway all the way to my room. She is not there, though I hear running water. I burst through the door only to find my mate on the ground with steam coming off her. I quickly kneel next to her. "Are you all right?" I ask, calming down as I feel her heal. She points toward the shower. "What is that?" I look to make sure where she is pointing. "The shower?" I ask, not sure what is happening. She nods, and my face heats up as I realize what it is. "It's to wash yourself. Does water harm you?" I ask, as I remember Claude saying that I can no longer swim in wolf form. She shakes her head. I could clearly see that it does. "No, I'm able to be in water," She says, then her face turns bright red as she whispers, "I just need to take my feathers off." My face is on fire as I realize what she means, not that I have never had those thoughts, but I don't think about them very often either. "Hmm, I, Hmm didn't know... hmm that you can do that." I stumble in embarrassment as my brain completely shuts off.

She, however, is laughing her head off. I can feel it's mainly out of embarrassment as well. She lifts up her arm, and it instantly lights on fire. As the fire dissolves it leaves bare skin. I grab her arm and kiss the now bare skin. "I'll go get you some shampoo and body wash." I get up and run out of the bathroom. I walk to the elevator, trying to calm myself down. I click onto the sub-basement where the storage is. There are three very large freezers and there are also fridges. Aisles of stuff like shampoo, conditioner, soap, deodorant, toothpaste, hair products, nail products, make up, and toothbrushes. It's literally like a store in here. I grab a bottle of shampoo in the scent of brown sugar and vanilla. I grab a bottle of body wash that is scentless. I head back to the room. I walk in with the soap. "Do you want to wear clothes or your feathers?" Okay, that is a very weird question to ask.

She looks deep in thought, "I would not mind some pants." I nod and head to go get her some. She looks to be my cousin's size. "Rose, can my mate borrow some pants?" I ask through the link. She responds, "Sure, what color?"

I don't know anything about matching colors or fashion. "I don't know, something that'll look good with white and gold." As I enter my office, a knock sounds on my office door. I open to see my cousin with a pair of skinny jeans, "Jeans go with anything," she says as she hands them to me. "Thank you, Rose," I say as I take the jeans, "No problem, she did rescue us," Rose says as she bows and leaves. I take the jeans to my room and lay them on the bed. I do not look toward the broken bathroom door. I quickly turn and walk out of the bedroom, gently closing the door behind me.

I go back to my office and look at the pack calendar. The pack game is in a few weeks. What am I going to do? This is the first pack game since I've been an alpha. We have a pack game every year to challenge the wolves and to get stronger as a pack since no wolf works alone. I'm currently mulling over this when I hear a door open in the background. "Asland are you in… oh there you are." I look behind me at the sound of my mate. Jaylen looks absolutely amazing, even with a towel on her head. "What are you doing?" she asks and I hand her the calendar. "The pack games are coming soon, and I've yet to come up with anything. Plus, getting attacked by my uncle didn't help matters." Jaylen looks to be pondering something. "Am I allowed to help?" She asks, and I'm dumbfounded. "Of course, you are allowed to help. You are my mate, my equal." She smiles and hands me back the calendar.

We are planning for a scavenger hunt race for the pack game. Jaylen is in charge of making the items and hiding them. I am in charge of making the groups and telling the rules. Everyone over five years old may play. Jaylen chooses a dinner with me as the reward for the winner. It is now the day of the pack game. "Jaylen, are you ready?" I ask through our mind link. "I got everything set on my side," Jaylen links back. I can hear her joy and excitement. "See you at the cliffs," I say with just as much excitement. I walk outside and let the fire roar to life. I shift into my fire wolf and run to the cliffs. I shift back and wait. "You know, you're going to give your mother a heart attack with this plan of yours." I smile at the sound of the most beautiful creature on the earth. "What can I say? I love keeping them on their toes." I turn and take her into a hug. "Darling, can you let go of me? This bag is getting a bit heavy."

I let go and noticed a big bag on her shoulder. "Are those the objects?" She nods, "All sixty of them." She sets the bag down and pulls out three different items. "There are twenty-three pieces of each, one for everyone in the game. My brothers had fun making them." She starts laughing, "They even named the items after themselves. This one is called Ashore." She holds up a fire ruby pendant with orange and yellow feathers on a gold chain. As as she puts it around my neck, she explains, "This is called Chalet." This time she holds up a deep sapphire pendant with green and purple feathers on a silver chain. "And last but not least, this one is called Jasper." She holds out a simple black pendant with red feathers on a black chain. Once all three of the pendants are on my neck, she shifts.

I tie the bag around her neck and climb onto her back. This is the third time I've been on her back. She walks to the edge and drives off. The first time she did this, it scared the daylights out of me. She soon rights herself and flies toward the cliffs. She soon lands and lies down so I can get off. As soon as I untie the bag, she shifts once more. She hands me ten of each. Then we go throughout the territory, hiding them in bushes, in the trees, and in the fallen leaves. After we are done, we meet back up at the cliff. I look at my watch. Mitchell should be bringing the pack now. Jaylen grabs the pendants, pulling my head down. She smiles and kisses me. "See you in a bit." With that, she jumps off the cliff. The orange glow lets me know that she is now in her phoenix form.

Soon after, Mitchell appears with everyone five and up. Normally, the pack games are only for fifteen and up, but Jaylen felt bad for the children so she made it to where five and up are able to play. After everyone is standing still, I split everyone up into twenty groups of three. There were ten five-year olds. Every child who can't shift has at least one adult wolf. "Okay, so this year's pack game is a scavenger hunt race. There are three pendants. Ashore." I hold out the ruby pendant on my neck. "Chalet." I hold the sapphire pendant. "And Jasper. Here are the rules. One, each group most have one person in human form at all times. Two, no stealing or foul play. Three, you must have all three objects and members at the finish line. Four, there will be no linking outside of your group. Five, have fun. The first group to win will be rewarded with a three dinners with me and my family. Each of the three winning members will choose one of the three meals.

After I finish explaining the game, I jump off the cliff. The wind rushes under me. "Asland!" I hear Mitchell yell out. I look down and see Jaylen fly under me. I land on the end of her neck. Both of my legs are on either side of it. I grab onto the antennas like feathers. She flies straight up. "See you guys at the pack house!" I shout out as she passes them. She flies above the trees. Soon, I see the pack house. She starts to glide down. Once she lands, she lies down, letting me climb off. Once I am off, she shifts. "So now what?" Jaylen asks as she walks up to me. "We watch the pups and wait." She smiles and grabs my right arm. I walk with her to the nursery. She instantly goes and plays with the pups. "She's already a wonderful luna, and she's ours," Claude says proudly.

Lilly jumps into my arms. "Aszy who's the girl with you?" Lilly asks pointing to Jaylen who's currently holding a one-year old pup. "Well, Lil, that's my mate and future luna." Lilly goes wide eyed. "Really! I want to meet her." Lilly pushes me to let her go. Once I set her down, she races over to Jaylen. Lilly pulls lightly onto one of Jaylen's tail feathers. I hope she's not hurt. Jaylen looks startled but not hurt. "Oh, hello dear. You must be Lilly." Jaylen lays the pup back in his bed and kneels down to Lilly's level.

Lilly gives a bright smile. "Yes, and you're the new luna." Jaylen looks slightly shocked and looks at me. She then rolls her eyes and smiles at Lilly. What was with the eye roll? "Dude, you didn't tell her that you were an alpha," Claude answers. Crap, I forgot to mention that. Jaylen starts playing with Lilly. I sit down on one of the couches and relax.

Soon, I feel a soft air ball hit my face and the room fills with laughter. I open my eyes to find the culprit holding her stomach laughing. I let out a playful growl. "Everyone, protect the luna!" Lilly yells, and instantly I'm attacked by balls coming from everywhere. I start chasing the pups and Jaylen. After a while, I finally catch Jaylen. Just as I catch her, the alarm at the finish line goes off. I let her go, and we walk out of the house hand in hand. The winning team consists of Dalton, May, and Amnia.

DINNER

Dalton is Mitchell's little brother, and May is his baby sister. There's also Amnia. Dalton has all the pendants on his neck. Mitchell, John, and Jill came right behind them. Jill is the one with the pendants. Soon all the pack arrives, and I announce the winner. Everyone immediately notices Jaylen, who is standing proudly by my side. I feel the pack's confusion. "I know that everyone is confused by this lovely lady here by my side. So, without further ado, let me introduce my mate and your luna, Jaylen."

At first shock goes through the pack and then joy, and the pack cheers and howls in joy. I notice at a few of the girls frown, but I ignore them. Jaylen looks very happy with the acceptance of the pack. "The winning team can meet me in my office after lunch. Everyone can dismiss." I grab Jaylen's hand and walk into the house. We get to my elevator. I turn on the hand scan and click add print. I then let Jaylen choose which hand to scan. She chooses her right and places it on the scanner. Once the light of the scanner goes from red to green, she removes it.

She then replaces it to open the elevator doors. Once they are open, we enter and I click on the tenth floor. When we arrive on my floor I grab, her hand and head to the kitchen. "What would my beautiful mate want for lunch?" I ask. Jaylen smiles, "May your beautiful mate have chicken cordon bleu?" I smile at her. "Oh, a good choice my dear. I will start right away." I give her a mock bow, making her laugh. I turn and start to gather the ingredients. Luckily, I've made it a couple of times. After gathering all of the ingredients, I preheat the oven to 350 degrees.

After forty-five minutes, lunch is done. I hand Jaylen a plate and set my plate next to hers. As I sit down, she takes a bite. "Yum, this is heavenly. You are now my personal chef." She smiles. "Oh, and here I thought I was your mate," I say. She gives a teasing smile. "You are and you belong only to me." She kisses my cheek. "As you belong only to me." I grab her chain and kiss her. She freezes in shock at first but then kisses me back. I pull away with a smile. We finish eating, and I walk to my office to wait for the winning team. Meanwhile, Jaylen decides to explore the library.

It isn't long until a knock sounds on my office door. "Come in," I call out and Dalton, May, and Amnia enter the room. "Good afternoon, Alpha." Dalton greets with his head low out of respect May also has her head lowered, but Amnia only slightly lowers her head. She's too proud for her own good. "Good afternoon, please sit down and we'll discuss your reward." Dalton and May sit on the farthest couch in the room. Amnia sits in a chair right next to my desk. "Okay, so each of you get to choose one meal for a day. You guys can discuss if you want to eat individually or as a...." Amnia interrupts me. "We will eat individually!" I let out a low growl. "One, don't interrupt me, and two, that's not your decision to make. It's between all three of you."

"Alpha, may I speak?" May asks timidly. I nod for her to continue. "If it's okay if only me and Dalton eat together...." Amnia growls at May and I growl at her. May shakes in fear. "May, please continue." With tears in her eyes, I can tell she mind-linked her brother. "She wants eat with just me and her for two days and Amnia can have her day by herself," says Dalton. He glares at Amnia because she scared May. Mitchell and his brothers are very protective of May. I really don't want to be with Amnia, but I can see why they don't want to eat with her.

"Yes, that is all right if everyone agrees." Amnia frowns, "But they get two days, while I get one." I sigh- I don't want to handle her drama right now. "Yes, because each person gets to choose a meal. You want to do yours individually, so you only get one meal on one day." I stand up, "If you want , you can have tonight's dinner." She instantly cheers up. Truth be told, I just want it to be done and over.

I dismiss them, and Amnia bolts ou,t probably to get ready. I walk out of my office and into the library. I walk around until I see Jaylen sitting at the widow with her nose stuck in a book. I walk up to her, I gently lift her up bridal style, I sit down where she was ,and I set her on my lap. She jumps a little before relaxing again. "We have dinner with one of the winners tonight. Her name is Amnia." Jaylen turns the page of the book and nods. "What will we be eating?" She asks as she closes the book. "I don't know yet." She nods and walks out of my arms and gets a new book.

We stay in the library until it was time for dinner. Jaylen reads most of the time while I just hold her. I walk out of the library and into the kitchen to prepare dinner. Amnia mind-linked me to what she wanted to eat, which is fish. It turns out Jaylen can't really handle fish very well, so I make her a pork chop. My family decides that they want to stay with the rest of the pack, so it is just the three of us. I sit the plates down ontohe table.

Jaylen sits down where the pork is and Amnia sits where the salmon is, which is the seat farthest from me. I sit down and started to eat. I notice that Amnia is getting very close. I can tell Jaylen also notices this because of the deadly glare. Amnia seems to ignore Jaylen's glare and comes even closer. I start to growl loudly at Amnia. She ignores it and continues. Right when Amnia touches me, Jaylen loses it. She grabs Amnia by the neck and pushes her against the wall. "Don't ever touch my mate," she demands.

DUEL

Amnia shakes in fear, which is the last thing she should do. "I'm his mate, not you." Amnia kicks Jaylen in the stomach, sending her back a little bit. I growl and go to attack, but Jaylen holds her arm out, telling me to stay out of it. "Are you challenging me?" Amnia's eyes widen, probably thinking Jaylen knows nothing about our system. "Yes, I, Amnia Johnson, challenge you, Jaylen What's Your Face, for the luna position."

Jaylen straightens, "I, Jaylen Ruby Firerose, accept your challenge." For an instant, I see a spark of fire on her antennae feathers. Shit just got real. "You have no idea what you have just done. Amnia Johnson, once this is over, you will kiss this pack goodbye." Amnia runs out of the kitchen and down the hall toward the office. Jaylen turns and faces me. Instead of her beautiful blue eyes, they are now ruby red with golden flames in place of the pupils.

Instantly, her normal blue eyes return and she smiles at me. "When will this duel take place?" She asks confidently, as though she has done this many times. "Just how many times have you done this?" I ask, curious about how the phoenixes live. "Well, I've been dueling since I was ten, when my mom announced me the next queen. There weren't very many duels, since many phoenixes wanted the queen to have a daughter. But several phoenixes wanted to marry my brothers, and if I wasn't there, then my mom would have to go to her daughter in-laws. So, I was challenged a bit, but Ruby wouldn't let us lose."

"Wait, wasn't Ruby alive before you were ten? Why didn't the others already know that you were the princess?" I ask, trying to understand Jaylen's world like she does with mine. "My mom kept me hidden until you were born. Ruby told her that you were born and she needed to find you. She came back three weeks later with knowledge of your name, place, and race. It's very rare to be mates with anyone but a dragon, griffin, and human. When I was fourteen, Ruby finally give me your name and race. Ever since then, I read everything about werewolves so that when you found me, I wasn't ignorant about your race and rules."

Jaylen smiles at me. Phoenixes are very confusing. I return her smile and pull her into my arms. "Tomorrow at noon is when your duel will take place. Since you were the one challenged, you decide the rules and place." She smiles but then quickly frowns. "I have to go; Mom's calling me home. See you at noon tomorrow." She kisses my cheek and jumps out the kitchen window. In a flash, she is a phoenix and flies away. I walk to my room, take a shower, and go to bed.

I wake up early to sign the duel papers. Once this is done, I go down to have breakfast with the pack. When I get to the dining room, everyone is chatting about the duel. They are talking about how Amnia is a fool because doesn't seem like a normal bird shifter and has more power than what is on the surface. They already believe in Jaylen and know she's the true luna. I walk in and grab a plate. I feel a hand grab my arm. I turn and see Amnia. I glare at her and yank my arm free. I sit between John and Mitchell so Amnia can't sit by me.

I continue to stick close to John and Mitchell, leaving no room for Amnia to get close to me. Soon, the noon bell rings, signaling the time for the duel. Everyone heads outside to witness the fight between Amnia and my mate. Amnia enters the arena. Jaylen is nowhere in sight. "Looks like she ran away." I'm about to growl at her, but an angelic voice bursts in my head. Jaylen spoke before I could growl. "I'm right here." Jaylen walks out of the forest and into the arena.

"I'm going to beat you and show Asland that I'm his true mate and not some stupid weak bird shifter." Instantly, Jaylen's eyes become the ruby color from before and the gold feathers on her eyes light on fire. In fact. all of her gold feathers are on fire. Everyone in the pack gasps in surprise. "I AM NO

STUPID BIRD SHIFTER! I AM THE NEXT QUEEN OF THE PHOENIXES!" Ruby yells in anger.

I can see Amnia shaking in fear, but that doesn't stop her and her wolf from trying to fight back. Ruby doesn't even move to dodge her. The flames start to move unnaturally around her. Ruby starts to use the flames on her arm feathers as blades. The fight is so one-sided. In a last-ditch effort, Amnia shifts into her small gray wolf. Ruby laughs out loud and says, "So you want to fight in our natural forms? That is even better for me. I can't even use a third of my power in this form." With that fire, engulfs her. The pack starts to panic like I did at first until they see the beautiful fiery white and gold phoenix.

Everyone gasps once more, for this is their first time truly seeing her true form. The flames instantly enlarge and form into inferno tornadoes circling Ruby as she flies five feet into the air. Amnia freezes with her tail in between her legs. I see pure rage in Ruby's eyes. Ruby lets out a war cry. "Something doesn't feel right," Claude says with fear. I feel it, too. Something about her eyes and fire doesn't feel right. "You must calm her down!" I turn at the new voice. There, behind the pack, is a young woman around twenty years old or so. She had red and orange feathers on her arms and chest just like Jaylen, but unlike Jaylen, she has on a red skirt instead of pants.

"How do I do that?" I ask. The lady gives me a warm smile. "You are Asland, are you not?" she asks like she already knows the answer. "Yes, I am." She nods like I answered my own question. "You're her mate, stupid," she says. I don't know how to calm a phoenix. Wait, of course, I don't need to know how- just being her mate means that I can calm her down. I run toward her. The fire flies toward me like it is about to attack me, but then the flames instantly wrap around me like they are going to protect me. I run toward Ruby as the fire circles around me. Once I am close enough, I jump and grab onto her neck. Ruby instantly quiets down and the fire dies down as well.

PHOENIXES

Once all the fires have died down, Jaylen lands and lies down so I'm not hanging in the air. I let go of her neck and walk to the front of her head. Her eyes are back to their blue color. "Are you two all right?" I ask as I pet their head. "Yes, we are okay," Ruby replies, sounding very tired. "You did good, Asland, which I should've expected from Jaylen's mate." I turn and see the lady walking toward us. Jaylen's head flies towards the lady and her eyes go wide. The lady suddenly laughs. "Asland, I believe it is time for you to meet the family of this young phoenix." The lady suddenly bursts into flames, scaring those near her. She flies off but then stops to see if we're following. Jaylen lowers her head, inviting me onto her neck. I climb on and grab onto her antennas. Jaylen then takes off after the red phoenix. We fly above the clouds, and I'll tell you what- it was cold going through the clouds but warm above them.

"Hold on tight." Ruby says, and I can practically hear her smirking. In the corner of my eye, I see the red phoenix back in and dive down. Then, I feel Jaylen doing the same thing. I lie flat on her neck and let go of her antennas to hug onto her neck. She dives toward the earth. I look past her head and see the earth approaching fast. Claude howls in the thrill of it all. Jaylen opens her wings like a parachute, and so does the red phoenix. We glide to the surface of the earth.

"Are you okay, Asland?" Ruby asks as she lands. "Yes, I'm fine." She lowers herself so I can get off. Once I am off, she shifts. "Welcome back. Sorry that you couldn't be with your family for long." Jaylen grabs my hand and drags me around. Everything is made from beautifully carved stone. Even though I've been here for two weeks, I have only stood in the castle. I haven't met her family yet, since she didn't want to overwhelm me while I was still learning to control my new form. So, this is the first time I get to look around the town. All the girls are just like Jaylen with different colored feathers. In fact, the most common colors are red with yellow feathers. There are some orange with yellow and red with orange but not once do I see another white with gold, or any white at all, for that matter.

"Why aren't there any white feathers like yours?" I ask. Jaylen stops and looks at the other phoenixes. "White feathers are extremely rare. Especially with gold." She smiles, "That is another reason why my mother hid me." So not only is she the next queen, she is also an extremely rare phoenix. "As you probably have noticed, the common feather colors of phoenixes are red as the main color with orange or yellow paired with it. The uncommon but not rare are the orange main with yellow or red paired. Rare colors are yellow as the main with red or orange pair. Then, the extremely rare are the white with red, orange, or yellow. All of the royal phoenixes have gold feathers, although sometimes they lean more toward the orange coloring."

I look around and notice that all the men were red, orange, or yellow shirts. Jaylen must've noticed me staring. "It's the fire festival. All the men wear the colors of their phoenix." I look at my plain blue shirt. "Don't worry, my mom already has clothes for you. She's been waiting to meet you for a long time. Sixteen years in fact." She smiles and leads me to her house, well, castle is a better word for it. Once we got there, I am whisked away by four phoenixes into the room I was in before. The four phoenixes consist of an orange base with red, red base with yellow, red base with orange, and a yellow base with orange.

"Here you go, Fire Prince," the phoenix with the orange base and red secondary feathers hands me the uniform. I figure I should probably shower so I look for the bathroom. My jaw drops at the very large swimming pool. It is made out what looks to be obsidian. It also a bowl shape with a marble white fountain in the center of it. The fountain has four phoenixes with their wings up and water coming out of their mouths. If I didn't know better, I'd say this is a birdbath.

I set the clothes on the counter near the door and also find scentless shampoo and body wash. I quickly wash myself and change into the uniform. The uniform looks like the one I had when I turned into a fire wolf but slightly different without the only cape and with a vest and jacket. I change into it; it also has a belt to go over the jacket. It has three different ropes on my left shoulder. As soon as I'm done getting dressed, the four phoenixes come in. "Fire Prince, the queen and the royal family are ready to meet you," one of them says as they look at my wet hair. "Fire Prince, bend down for a moment." I smile and start following them. Claude howls in excitement, although I'm a bit nervous.

They guide me through a lot of very large halls to another room. At the far end of the room, there is the lady from before with four other guys. All four of them are glaring at me. My alpha instincts kick in, and I hold my head up proudly. Instantly, attitude of the the man closest to the lady changes. "Hello, Asland. If you haven't figured it out yet, I'm Rubeasta's mother, Queen Powlistia Firerose. This is her father, King John Firestorm, and her brothers, Princes Ashore, Chalet, and Jasper Firestorm."

Why did she use Ruby's full name instead of Jaylen? "Phoenixes go by the phoenix's name, for they are born first. Like how everyone calls you Asland and not Claude. It's just respectful, though you don't need to worry about that." Jaylen says, answering my question. "Where is Ruby?" They all look confused then it clicks. "Oh, she did say that you call her that. She's getting ready for the festival. We wanted to talk to you while we wait," Ashore says as he walks towards me.

As Ashore walks toward me, balls of Fire form in his hands. I stand my ground, not moving an inch. Crap, what do I do? Ashore throws the fireballs at me. I close my eyes and think of when Jaylen's fire wrapped around me as if to protect me. Instantly, I feel my body get warm. I open my eyes and see fire circling around me, just like before. "Well, that proves he's her mate when the fire tornadoes circle around him and block Ashore's attack." I think it was Jasper who says this. "No doubt about it," Chalet says, sounding very passive. "Geez Boys, I've already told you that he calmed the fire rage within her," her mom says, looking annoyed. After the Fire festival, we headed back to the pack house.

Jaylen starts to descend below the clouds, and I start to see the pack house. I lie flat against her. She instantly knows what I mean. She tucks in her wings and dives toward the pack house. This time, I let out a howl of joy. Jaylen opens her wings as a parachute again. Once Jaylen lands, she lies down. I slide off and watch as she shifts. She smiles and follows me to the elevator. I scan my hand and the doors open. We enter and click on our floor. Once the door closes, Jaylen grabs my neck and pulls my head down. She kisses me, and I instantly wrap my arms around her and kiss her back.

Once the doors open, I pick her up and she wraps her legs around my waist without breaking the kiss. I walk to my room and set her on to the bed. We break the kiss to breathe. I stare into her eyes which are full of love and joy. She grabs my neck again, but instead of kissing me, she whispers the words I longed to hear. "Mark me." I pull away to make sure that I'm not dreaming. "Are you sure?" She nods and exposes her neck. I feel Claude coming to the surface, but this time not to take control.

I feel my canines grow sharper as I kiss down her neck until I found the spot where my I will place my mark. Once I find it, I bite down, piercing the skin. She lets out a short scream of pain then moans in bliss as the special toxins in my saliva enter her bloodstream. "I love you, my beautiful wolf." I take out my canines and lick the wound clean, healing it. "I love you, too, my fiery bird." With that, I know she is asleep. Every time a female is marked, they fall asleep as it takes a lot of energy out of them. I smile and wrap my arms around her. I kiss my new mark and allow sleep to take me.

NOT A DREAM

I wake up and Jaylen was gone. Did I dream that or was it real? I turn onto my back and stare at the ceiling. "Oh, good, you're awake. I made you breakfast." I smile at the sound of her voice. I'll never tire of hearing it. I turn over and see her. She has her hair in a ponytail and her antennas are free, but what catches my eye is her neck. She bares my mark. The mark turned into a tattoo-like form instead of a bite mark. The mark is a wolf howling to the moon and a phoenix flying over it, and under this is written "Asland and Jaylen."

"Admiring your handiwork?" Jaylen asks as she puts a tray of food on my lap. "I am indeed." I gently brush my hand over the mark, sending shivers down her spine. She smiles and says, "Now eat your food," through the mind link we formed. "Fine, it smells great." I reply back through the mind link. I look at the food, and it looks like charcoal. I ignore the look of it, cut a piece, and put it in my mouth. Instantly, an unfamiliar taste enters my mouth. It is amazing and has a fiery kick to it.

"What is this?" I ask, taking another bite. "It's charstemia. It's a phoenix breakfast when they need a lot of energy for a long flight. I know being alpha is very draining, so I made this for you." After a few minutes, I feel better than ever. It was better than drinking an energy drink. "Alpha, Alpha Holden and Alpha Boston are here for the rogue meeting today," Mitchell mind-links me. I put my hand against my forehead. Crap, I forgot about that. "I have a meeting to go to. Do you want to come or do something else while I'm in the meeting?" I ask as I jump out of bed and into my closet to change. "I'll hang out with your mom and sister," she tells me

I hear the door open and close. I finish getting dressed and head to the office. Just as I walk in, my elevator opens, revealing the two other alphas. How did they get in there? "The luna let us in when she walked out. She said you were waiting and to come up." She made it sound like I didn't forget and overslept. "I've never seen a luna like her. If it is all right to ask, what is her species? She is very special," asks Alpha Boston. Then, I mind-link Jaylen, "The other alphas are wondering what species you are, is it all right if I tell them?"

"I don't care. The information that phoenixes want hidden is long forgotten. Go right ahead." Information they wanted hidden, what is that? I'll ask her later. I turn to the other alphas. "She is a phoenix. Anyways, shall we get this meeting on the way?" I guide them to the meeting room. We discuss cases with rogues, which are abnormal at the moment, and then argue about the same old information like we always do.

Finally, the meeting is over. I bid them goodbye as they enter the elevator. After finishing the paperwork for the end of the meeting, I decide to go in search of my mate. She somehow ended up training the wolves. I don't know how that happened. "Jaylen, how in the world did this happen?" Jaylen turns toward me and smiles. She turns back to the training wolves. "At ease. You can go get a drink and rest." Instantly, everyone drops to the ground, exhausted. What in the world did she do? Even Mitchell and John look dead tired.

Jaylen turns and hugs me. "Mitchell was training the wolves, and I said that I could train my brothers twice as hard. He told me to prove it. So that's how it happened. Just in case you were wondering." I look at my pack. It looks like she made it equal for both male and female members. "You have one evil trainer of a mate," Mitchell says through the pack link. Everyone groans in agreement. Jaylen turns back to the pack. "Now, shall we continue?"

I look at them. "You know, it might be better to start on the lowest level while starting a new form of training," I say, hoping to help them. "Of course, I know that! That's why I'm working on the basics with everyone." Everyone jumps up and runs out of the field and into the house. "Oh dear, look at all that energy they still have." Just what kind of training did Jaylen do?

"Mitch, are you okay?" I ask through the mind link. "No man. I'm going to have nightmares about this for the rest of my life." I sigh, "It couldn't have been that bad." Mitchell opens his mind and shows me his memories. Let's just say what I saw was a complete nightmare. Mitch and the pack were chased by fire. Every exercise involved fire. The fires seemed to be different from one other. There were all different sizes and colors.

I pale as the memory disappears. No wonder he said he's going to have nightmares. I turn toward my smiling mate. She is so kind and innocent; she couldn't do that. It had to be Ruby. "Lunch time," Jaylen says and hugs me, giggling. I smile and put the memory of the training in the back of my mind. We head to my kitchen to make lunch. I doubt the pack wants to see Jaylen at the moment. Once in the kitchen, Jaylen asks for a simple ham and cheese sandwich with a salad. I make her sandwich as she smiles and watches me.

I put her sandwich in front of her and go to make mine. She sits up and kisses my cheek. I frown and grab her chain. I make her look up at me and kiss her lips. She immediately kisses back. I deepen the kiss until we have to catch our breath. I smile and go to make my sandwich. I finish making my sandwich and sit next to her. I kiss her cheek and start to eat my sandwich. We talk and laugh. Nothing can take this happiness from me, I think to myself.

Fire of Death

It's now been a week after I've marked Jaylen, and it's been the happiest time in my life. Lilly has grown very fond of Jaylen and so has the rest of the pack. Though the pack feared Ruby's training at first, they always go back and have her train them more. In fact, I had to join, too. I tried my hardest not to, but Ruby refuses to let me off the hook. She said that because I'm her mate, I had to do the training even more so than the pack. Let me tell you, it was a nightmare. I am not immune to this fire. She calls it the inner flame. She draws the fire from you. Ruby isn't the trainer- the fire is your trainer. The fire knows your limitations, strengths, and weaknesses. Everyone has become a lot stronger. I'd like to see the rogues attack us now.

Right now, I'm doing paperwork. Jaylen is lying on the couch, reading a book. Jaylen left a couple of times. She usually comes back with snacks for me and her. "Jaylen, do you want to go get some air with me?" I ask, wanting to get out of the office. "Sure, I'd love to." She puts a bookmark in and sets the book down. She gets up and walks up to me. I sign the paper I am on and set the pen down. I get up and grab her hand. We walk into the elevator and click the first floor.

We exit the elevator and head outside. Jaylen sees mom and heads over to her. "Hi Ma, how are you?" Mom turns and smiles. "Jay dear, it's so lovely to see you. I'm doing just great. How are you two doing?" I smile at her, "we're good. In fact, we're going on a walk to get some air." Mom smiles and wishes us well. I grab Jaylen's hand and head to the woods.

Walking through the woods with Jaylen is very nice. Jaylen always stops to smell the flowers. "Asland, where are we going?" I shrug, "Nowhere really. Just walking and enjoying the nice weather instead of being cooped up in that stuffy office all day." She gives me an evil grin. "We could always train." A chill goes down my spine. The new training is great at getting us physically strong but very bad for us mentally.

"You said that you'll only train us three times a week." She nods, "But that's only for the pack. You, on the other hand, need even more training then they do." Ruby's voice comes out at the end. She rubs her hand against my chest. "Through I believe you're very strong, you've not yet reached your potential." Ruby purrs in my ear. Man, she's makes me crazy. I step back and grab her chain. "Ruby, you are a crazy hard trainer, but that's what I like about you." I lean in and kiss her.

She pulls back and gives a warm smile, showing that Jaylen has reappeared. "Let's continue our walk." She smiles and hooks arms with me. I love how peaceful the forest is- the birds chirping, the gentle wind blowing into the leaves, the squirrels scurrying about in the trees, and my beautiful mate beside me. What could go wrong?

Suddenly, Jaylen jumps in front of me. Instantly, the world goes in slow motion as Jaylen lets out a scream of pain. I also feel unbearable pain in the center of my chest. I soon see a piece of metal protruding out of her back. That's when it hits me. Jaylen was shot with a silver tip arrow. A golden flame engulfs her. It wasn't her shifting flame. It disappears instantly with a blast.

I fall to my knees at a pile of ashes with a broken arrow on either side of the pile. With tears in my eyes I scoop up some of the ashes. "Please no, no, no. NO!" I let out a howl of pain and mourning. I sit there, letting the tears fall because my world has shattered. My sun has fallen, my soul is broken, and my heart is shattered. The forest is deadly silent as though it is mourning also. The gentle breeze brushes away the ash.

Panic clenches my heart. I quickly tear off my shirt and start scooping her ashes into it. I'm trying my hardest to gather all of it up. Once I feel like I can't get anymore, I tie my shirt around the ashes so the wind can't take them away. I pick up the shirt and hug it as my heart breaks again. I feel many mind-links trying to contact me to find out why I'm mournful for they aren't yet connected to Jaylen. I block them and just sit there, numb to my surroundings. Even when it starts to rain, I stay frozen in the spot.

I slowly get up and head back to the house. The rainstorm is mirroring my heart. My feet drag in the muddy ground as I walk to the pack house. The shirt is clenched between my arms. I get home and do not care that I'm bringing mud into the house. I just walk to the elevator. I go to scan my hand and see it covered in dirt and ash. My mate's ashes. Tears once again sting my eyes as they pour out. The doors open and I walk in. I click the tenth floor and lean my head above the panel and return my arm around the ashes.

The elevator's doors open. I walk into the dark office. A flash of lightning lights it up. The desk is once again full of papers to be read and signed. I ignore them and walk to the hallway and enter an empty room. I set the shirt down on the floor and went into the control room. Opening the list, I turn off my elevator and all electricity on my floor. I then go into the kitchen and grab the small table. I drag it into the room with her ashes. I put the table in the center of the room. I grab her and lie her onto the table. I untie the soaking wet shirt and am surprised to find the ashes dry.

BROKEN

I fall to my knees. "Why did you jump in front of me?" I let my body fall in despair. I put up a mental wall blocking everyone, even my own wolf. Soon my eyes burn from all the crying and exhaustion. I close them and let darkness take me. I'm immediately greeted by trees and the sound of birds. "Asland, let's continue our walk." I turn and see her smiling face. She grabs my hand and we walk.

I smile, enjoying the peace of the forest. Her laughter and voice bring me unimaginable joy. Suddenly, she jumps in front of me and screams. A golden flame engulfs her and disappears. I shoot up, screaming in pain as my heart shatters even more. I look at my phone and realize it's two in the morning. I put it back in my pocket and look at the black ashes on the table. Normally ashes are light gray or even tan. I don't know how long I sit here staring at the ashes wishing for them to move and turn back into their original living form. I suddenly feel someone trying to get in contact. It's not Claude, so it must be Mom, Dad, or Mitchell. I ignore it as it slowly fades away. Then my phone goes off. I guess they haven't decided to give up. I pull out my phone and see that it's Mom and it's also noon. I've been staring at the ashes for ten hours.

I let it ring and then turn off my phone. I lay down and stare up at the table. My eyes become heavy and I let them close. This time Jaylen is in front of me. Her back is covered in blood, staining her beautiful white back feathers. She turns around and faces me. Her face is pale and her breathtaking green eyes are lifeless. "Why did you let me die?! You were supposed to protect me!" She cries out, her voice is full of pain. "I'm sorry. I'm so sorry." She disappears and I wake up with tears in my eyes.

I crawl over to the table and stand up. "I'm so sorry my love. You are my everything. The air I breathe, the light, the warmth of the sun, and the other piece of my soul. I was incomplete before meeting you and now I'm nothing but a waste of space. An empty shell of who I was supposed to be. I couldn't protect you. I've failed you as a mate." I fall to my knees. I don't know how long it has been. I suddenly hear banging outside the room. I push myself off the floor and slowly stand. I shift into my morning form and look into the mirror. My form looks normal, though I've got red stripe down my neck and large spot on my chest. Luckily, the flames are very low with exhaustion and pain. I slowly walk out the room and close the door behind me. I follow the banging to my office. Once I reach my office ,the door is thrown off its hinges. There, huffing and puffing, is my mom's brown wolf. She shifts and gives me a glare full of anger, pain, fear, and worry.

"Get in the shower now, while I make you something to eat." I nod and slowly walk to the bathroom in my room. As I shift into my human form, as not to harm myself farther. I take my clothes off and let the water run over my skin. I don't do anything else. After a while, I feel I've been in long enough to exit the bathroom and change into my morning form, as well as clean clothes. I walk to the kitchen and see a plate on the counter. I walk up and sit. It has two eggs and toast. I really don't want to eat but I humor my mom and slowly ate. After finishing an egg and half of the toast, I can't eat anymore.

Mom watches my every move. Once she sees I'm not going to eat any more, she takes my plate and washes it and puts it in a box. She then starts boxing my knives, forks, glass objects, and anything else she sees as a possible way for me to harm myself. She even looks like she wants to take the oven so I didn't light myself on fire, which almost made me laugh since I'm immune to fire. I don't have the strength to tell her I'm not going to kill myself. I just lie my head on my arms and fall back to sleep.

It's been a whole miserable week and four days since Jaylen's death. I'm tormented by her death. Every-night I see her back pierced with an arrowhead and her pain-filled screams, and the deadly golden flames awake me with a cold sweat. Many times, she turns around and asks why I allowed her to die. Her face is pale white with an arrow pierced in her chest. I rarely eat and rarely sleep. I allow no one near her ashes or even in the room she's in. Mom also turned the elevator back on and my Dad took over my alpha duties for me until I can take them back. My mom also comes and makes me food every day.

I lie still in my bed. I glance at the alarm clock. It is three in the morning, signaling another day without Jaylen. I crawl out of bed and walk into the bathroom. I'm no longer skin and bones like a week ago, though my blue eyes are even more lifeless than before. My fur is matted and unclean. I turn away from my reflection. I walk out of my room and notice a light shining through the cracks of the door of the room where Jaylen's ashes are located. I walk up to it and slowly turn the door knob, thinking that I must've left the lights on. I open the door and freeze. Jaylen's ashes turned to gold and are glowing; some are even floating around the room. I slam the door shut in disbelief. I slowly walk into the kitchen and sit at the table. I put my arms on the table and my head on them as the tears pour out.

I hear a light knocking at the door. I turn and see my mom. "Bear, do you want me to make you something?" I turn and put my head back onto my arms. "Do whatever you want," I mumble/ I know she is going to make me eat no matter what I say or do. Soon, I hear pots and pans. I can now eat a full meal, but I never eat like before, and I've forbidden mom from making me chicken cordon bleu. I start to smell beef. I soon hear a plate set by my head. I lift up my head and see a steak with a salad. Mom hands me a fork and a knife.

It is Time for War

My mom closely watches me so that I don't decide to use the knife to kill myself. She's gotten less sleep than I have since she's constantly checking up on me. I feel bad for her; she's constantly afraid of finding me dead somewhere. Even though I don't feel like living anymore, I could never hurt her like that. She doesn't deserve it and neither does the pack. I will let nature take its course, even if I wish for it to hurry up and take me to her. My mind also wanders to Jaylen's ashes? How could they float around the room and glow gold? No, tellingg myself I must be hallucinating since I haven't slept well in days. I shake my thoughts away and start eating. Mom slowly eats her steak and salad. I notice her glancing at my arms trying to see if I have cut myself with my claws, I guess. She takes the knifes once we are done with them and packs then again when she finishes cleaning them.

Then she stares daggers at my shirt. I sigh and stand up. I pull my shirt off showing her my chest and back. "Mom, even though my world is gone, my sun is dead, and my soul is broken, I would never hurt you or the pack that way. I will not harm myself with my own hands." She looks into my eyes and tears up. I know exactly what my eyes look like and why she is so scared. I put my shirt back on and sit down. Mom puts her hand on my cheek. "I'm sorry my pup. I'm just so scared of you joining her by k..ki...killing yourself." She breaks down into tears. Very few members actually know that Jaylen is dead. I've tried getting ahold of the phoenixes; they have yet to answer any of my calls. Nobody knows that my dad is actually doing the pack work except for me, mom, Mitchell, and John. I pick up the knife and fork and start eating again.

I hear footsteps running up the hallway. I turn and see Mitchell dent down to catch his breath. "We. Found. The. Rogue. Pack. And. One. Of. Them. Had. A. Very. Bad. Burn. On. His. Arm." Mitchell says after every breath. Rage instantly fills me as I let out a growl, making my mom jump. "Where?" I ask. Mitchell straightens, "They are East of Bloodstone Pack. The Bloodstone Pack has offered to help and is ready to join us." I walk to my office with Mitchell following close behind. I see my dad isn't in the room. I grab a map. They're about two weeks away, but it will only take one week for an enraged wolf. "How many rogues are there?"

"There are about thirty, and there was one that looked in charge of them." Mitchell hands me pictures of the rogue pack. The last picture is of a single male. In the angle of the picture, you can definitely see that his left arm is very badly burned. I bolt out of the office door, jumping down the flight of stairs. I don't care that the elevator would have been faster. I just need to move. By time I am on the first floor, Mitchell and the pack warriors are waiting and ready for war. I bolt past them and shift into my fire wolf for the first time since Jaylen's passing. My pack looks at me in shock as the fire within me flares in rage. I ignore them and start running to the Bloodstone Pack. They instantly shift and run after me.

I open the pack link slightly and am instantly hit with the pack's rage and determination. It hits me that no one needs to be told their luna is dead. They already know and wanted revenge just like I did. I stop at the area where the trees and the ground are scarred by the golden flames of death and let out howl of war the pack join. It is time for this war to begin.

PAIN UNTIL REBIRTH

I open my eyes, and I quickly sit up and feel around my chest where the arrow pierced me. I notice that I feel no pain. I look around. I'm in a cave in a nest. This looks familiar, though I can't really see since it's so dark here. It suddenly brightens as a white and gold phoenix appears at the entrance. "Hello, Jaylen." Ruby greets me. I run up and hug her. "We forgot to tell our mate something very important." I look at her a little confused. Ruby turns her head towards the wall with the mirror. I follow her gaze to see Asland crying over my ashes. I run to the wall, "I'm alright, I'll return soon!" I yell through the link. "It's no use. We don't have enough energy to communicate with him." Ruby says, the pain clear in her voice. I fall to my knees as I see him scream in agony. I even feel it in the core of my being. I wrap my arms around my knees and cry. "This is all my fault, I should have told him." I feel Ruby lie her head next to me. I watch as Asland scoops up my ashes as the rain starts to fall. My heart shatters as I see how broken he is. I watch him as he forces himself to move, my heart breaking with each step.

I see him untie the shirt with my ashes. He looks a little surprised to see them still dry. "See I'm still here. There is still life in those ashes!" I yell with tears in my eyes, even though I know he will not hear me. I watch as he falls to his knees. "Why did you jump in front of me?" His voice sounds so broken. "I'm so sorry. I'm so sorry that I forgot to tell you." I see his body fall and I panic, but Ruby doesn't flinch at the sight. "Is he all right?" I ask with tears pouring out like a dam broke. "Mentally no, not at all. Physically, he is okay, but not for long," she answers, her voice seems calm but I know that it's anything but calm.

"We need to find his wolf." I run to the edge of the cave and see a steep cliff. The spirit realm mirrors that of the mortal realm. Ruby comes up from behind and lies down so I can get on. As soon as I'm on, she takes off. We fly toward the pack to the north. It's a very short flight. She lands, and I see a lot of the wolves of the pack, though I don't really know who their human counterparts are. I search for one in particular. I soon find him staring at the water in a pond near the pack house. "Claude!" I shout with joy. He turns; at first, he looks extremely angry, but then his eyes widen as he sees both me and Ruby. "What is happening here?" he asks as we get closer to him. He seems to also be in denial, so I send him my joy and relief at seeing him, as well as my regret at what I have caused. He runs toward us. I wrap my arms around him and cry into his fur. "How are you two here?" he asks, as the truth settles in his heart. "There is only one way to permanently kill a phoenix and that's to kill their mates. So, instinctively, I jumped in front of you before I even knew why." His flames burn brighter with joy then dim with pain. "I wish I could tell Asland but he has blocked everyone, even me," Claude says with so much pain that I cry harder.

I cry as I feel Asland's pain. I focus all my strength and scream at the wall blocking me from my mate. I try again and again to get through and comfort him. I constantly yell I love you and not to give up. I hear every word he says, like that he is a terrible mate, which breaks me even more. "You will never fail me as long as you live!" I shout as I fall to my knees. I'm not sure how long I've been in the spirit realm, but I know that it will take me two weeks to return. I'm just glad that he isn't suicidal right now. I still have time. I stare at the wall with the mirror; Asland is currently eating with his mom when Mitchell bursts in. "We. Found. The. Rogue. Pack. And. One. Of. Them. Had. A. Very. Bad. Burn. On. His. Arm." Mitchell says after every breath. My heart drops; this is the last thing Asland needs. I feel his rage and his need for revenge. "Don't do it!" I yell, pounding against the mirrored wall. He runs out of the kitchen and down the stairs. "Please Asland, don't do this!" I cry as I know that he has no ties to life. "ASLAND!" I yell with all of my strength, and the next thing I know, I'm running off a cliff. I shake my head as pain shoots throughout my body. My eyes widen. You can't feel pain when in the spirit realm. I look around. It isn't a cliff I ran off of, it is a table. I'm back! I force myself to get up through the pain and run to the wall. I need to hurry. I don't have much time. I can see that the moon is high in the sky.

I melt the window so I can fly out. As soon as it is melted, I try to fly, only to not leave the ground whatsoever. I look at my wings; they are just fluffy sticks. Crap, I don't have time for this. I speed up the regeneration process on my wings by focusing on them. Normally Ruby would be helping with this, but she is in the spirit realm with Claude trying to get ahold of Asland. As soon as my wings are partially there, I take off. I see that the moon is now setting. I have got to hurry.

I make it over the windowsill before my wings give in. I tumble to the roof and roll a few times. I sigh as I stop just a hair's length from the edge. I'm not usually afraid of heights, but this is terrifying. I get up and take off. I don't get far, as the wind blows too hard for my still-forming wings to handle. The wind slams me into a tree. My body screams for me to stop while my soul and heart screams to hurry. I can feel that Asland has no will to make out of this fight. I light up my wings in determination and glare at the invisible wind. It's not going to keep me from my mate. I take off, and the wind hits me hard and blows out my flames. I slam into a tree once again. I light my wings up again and take to the sky. I get up and fight again and again before my wounds fully heal. Each time it is getting easier as my wings grow in length and strength.

After slamming against the third tree, the wind no longer seems as strong. I can now fly against the wind but I have to rest every five minutes. The sun is rising just over the horizon. I feel that my mate is still asleep. I need to hurry. I start to fly again. As the sun rises higher, I feel Asland stir. I try to comfort him with the feelings of peace. I'm not sure if he gets them, but it doesn't matter. I will make it to him. I push my wings to their limit and quickly land before I fall. I have been moving for twenty minutes but barely covered any ground. I would have made it to Asland even before the sunrise with my old wings. However, I have barely gotten past Asland's pack borders with these baby wings. I rest for a moment before flying once more.

I continue to push my limit to get to Asland as fast as I can. After a long time and many rests, I can feel the connection is stronger. I feel pure rage course through my body. He has found the rogues. I'm running out of time. I launch myself off the branch. I start to get tried just as I see a battle. Based on all of the beautiful wolves and all of the matted ones, I know this is it without seeing my mate. I light up every single matted wolf there is. This makes me lose the last of my energy, and I start to fall. However, as I fall, my energy starts to quickly come back to me. I'm getting closer to my mate. I steer myself toward my black and orange wolf. He is standing with the others in an ash-covered field. I try to slow down but am unable to and I crash into the back of my mate's head. I made it; I curl into his fur in relief.

<h1 style="text-align:center">REVENGE AND ASHES</h1>

With the pack's rage, we make it to Bloodstone Pack by nightfall. We enter the territory and fall asleep near the pack home. Tomorrow is when we are going to get our revenge. I lay down and let sleep take me to my nightmares, but the nightmares never come. I wake up with the warmth of the sun shining on my fur. I sit up and groan as my body hurts all over, especially my back. I must have slept wrong. I shake out my sore muscles and stare at the clear sky as the sun rises. I'm at peace, and the fire within me is at rest. I stand up and shake out my fur. My pack warriors also start to stir. I take the time to see just who came with my beta and delta. There are four other warriors with John and Mitchell. "Good morning, Firestorm Pack. I have five of my top warriors ready to join you." The Bloodstone Alpha greets us. "Come and eat breakfast before we head out towards the rouges." I nod, as I shift into my morning form and follow the other alpha. My beta and warriors follow after me.

I freeze when I see everyone with their mates. I try my best to ignore the pain in my chest. Soon it will be all over. My pain and suffering will end at last. Mitchell comes and pats my back. "I'm always here for you, man," he says as he walks away.

It is now time to head out to war. I walk out of the Bloodstone Pack's house and shift. I let out a howl of war. Everyone howls with me. I'm going to get revenge for you, Jaylen, and then join you. I turn and see ten wolves who are ready to fight. I turn face to face with the Bloodstone Alpha. "May you lead us to victory." I nod and turn and head out with my wolves and the Bloodstone wolves. I feel the fire within me roar to life and am ready to fight. I let the fire come forth and walk into my new form. The pack jumps out of shock at my new form. I ignore it and head to the east. The warriors follow suit behind me.

Soon, an awful smell of rotten flesh greets my nose. We have arrived at the rogues' camp. I turn toward the warriors with my eyes ablaze and nod to the others to get ready. They nod back, telling me they already are. I let out a battle cry and charge into the rogue pack. The rogues turn in shock; many jump and run off, and others quickly shift to fight. They charge at us. Everything seems to go into slow motion. I see a wolf with all its fur burned off on its left foreleg. I'd know those burns anywhere. I feel my flames burst out of my coat. I can't see myself, but I knew that I am now a pure fire wolf. I charge at the wolf with the burned leg. The rogue freezes as he looks at me as if I am from a nightmare and tucks his tail in between his legs. I know that I have already won as I launch at his throat. Instantly, my flames devour him. Soon, the scent of burned fur and flesh hit my nose. I quickly drop the body that is now burnt to a crisp. Note to self: no more rough play with those who aren't flame-resistant. I feel my fur blanket my flames as I turn to see how the others are faring.

Time starts to slow yet again, as one by one the rouges burst into flames. I freeze in shock and so does everyone else. What just happened? The rogues instantly fall down into ashes. Everyone one turns and looks at me in question. "Dude, I wasn't going to ask until this was all over, so since it is now, what the hell happened to you?!' Mitchell yells through the general pack link. "And how on earth did you turn all the rogues to ashes?" another of my warriors asks. "The first question is a very confusing one. Let's just say my mate turned me into a flame wolf. As for the second question, I don't know. I don't even think it was me. I was too focused on killing the one that killed my mate," I answer via the general pack link. Suddenly, something small and light hits me on the back of my head. Mitchell shifts and bursts out laughing. "Dude, you got a bird on your head." Everyone in the Bloodstone Pack stares at him in shock, they can't believe Mitchell's disrespect toward his alpha. I carefully shift so the bird doesn't get hurt. I then gently grab it off my head. I move it in front of me. Instantly, I fall to my knees and cry. I don't even care if the others can see me.

The small bird rubs its head against my forehead, then it pecks my forehead very hard. I lift my head to see the tiny white and gold fluffball of a bird glaring at me. "Jaylen, you're so fluffy and tiny." She lets out a chirp as her eyes soften. "How is this possible?" I hold her in the palm of my hands. I feel someone is trying to break my walls down. I allow them to fall. I'm instantly greeted with her voice. "I was reborn. There is only one way to kill a phoenix." My eyes widen in surprise, "What is the one way to kill a phoenix?" I ask through the mind-link. She says two words that made everything fall into place. "Their mate."

I feel Claude enter my mind. "Finally! I've been trying to tell you that her soul was still connected to us for a while for two weeks. Next time, don't block me out. I am part of you and getting cut off from you hurts. Once with our uncle and now by you. You doing it on your own will hurt a whole lot more," he growls and then pulls away. "Do you have any idea of what I went through?!" Jaylen yells as tears fall down her cheeks and make a wet trail in her undeveloped feathers. Her feathers are like those of a chick. I am about to say the same thing back, only for her to put her head against my thumb, which is currently bigger than her head. Suddenly, Jaylen opens her mind and shows me her memories.

I instantly cried at how much she went through to get to me. "Thank you," is all I could say. "Asland, I was always with you. No matter how many times I die, I will return to you. No matter how far you are, I will do everything in my power to go and stand by your side. You and I are one. Even if you die, I will join you." She mind-links me as she rubs her tiny head on mine. I stand up with her asleep in my arms. "Let's head back." Everyone nods, and we walk back to the Bloodstone territory. It took a while since I stayed in human form, but there was no hurry.

"Welcome back. I heard that you guys didn't even fight all that much, and that all the rogues burst into flames. How is that possible?" the Bloodstone Alpha asks. I look at my baby phoenix. "My mate saved us the trouble." The alpha looks at me, clearly confused. "I thought your mate was killed by rogues." I smile, glad to be back to my old self. "So did I, but apparently phoenixes get reborn after two weeks if their ashes are not harmed." I added a slight lie to keep the truth from entering the wrong ears. "So I'm guessing the baby bird you have in your arms is your mate?"

I nod and the Bloodstone Alpha says, "Come and have lunch with us." My pack cheers, making the Bloodstone Pack laugh. I'm glad that the black cloud is gone from in my heart and over my pack, and we have this little fluff ball to thank for both the black cloud and for the light. We all enter the dining room. Mitchell gets me a plate since I have my hands full. Once he sets the plate in front of me, he goes to get his own. I gently shake Jaylen awake so she can get something to eat and she bites me. Her bright blue eyes glare at me as she curls back into a ball and goes back to sleep.

Bracelet of Rebirth

We head back to our pack in our wolf forms. Jaylen hitches a ride on my head. For the past week, Jaylen has been so tiny, but she now has all of her feathers, even though she is still only the size of a canary. I love having her being so tiny that she fits in the palms of my hands, but I really miss her human self. I also miss flying on her back. I'm currently walking while Jaylen is flying overhead. Soon, I feel her landing on my head. "Hello Jaylen," I greet through the bond. "Hey, how much longer to the pack?" She asks calmly, there are no complaints within her tone. "About another week at this pace." I answer as a crisp breeze blows, carrying the scent of winter with it. "Oh okay, oh and also I told my mom to come pick us up since I am currently unable to fly there by myself. My wings are too small for that height.' I nod and decide to find a place to camp. We soon find an open field. My warriors have gotten used to my new look, although they still jump every time I shift.

Everyone except for Jaylen is in human form. Jaylen is currently asleep on my shoulder. I explain to my pack that I'll be leaving them to help Jaylen. They will need to return home without me. As soon as I'm done explaining, I hear the shriek of a great bird. I guess Jaylen's mom is here. We all look up and see a red and gold phoenix. She slowly descends, giving us enough time to move out of the way. Jaylen chirps and lightly flips her wings. Jaylen's mom lowers her neck so I may climb up. I do so without question. As soon as I'm on, she lifts her head up. I quickly put Jaylen in my sweater pocket and grab onto the antennas that are thin and long like feathers. Jaylen looks a lot like her mother except for the white instead of red and also the tail feathers. Her mother has two very long ones while Jaylen has three. I nod to my warriors, 'Mitchell, be careful,' I say in the link. "You too, man," he says in reply. "I'm ready," I say to Jaylen's mom. I feel bad that I forgot her name. Jaylen's mom looks up and takes off.

"Will your brothers attack me again?" I ask jokingly through the mind link. "They most certainly will." The seriousness is very clear in her voice. I let out a groan, and she laughs. "Do not worry, they have no means to kill you." This time her voice is very playful and happy. "Of course not, why would they kill their beloved baby sister." We both burst out laughing. We fly in a peaceful silence, enjoying each other's company. After some time, Jaylen speaks. 'Ready?' Jaylen didn't need to explain for what. I immediately lie flat against her mom's neck. She tucks in her wings and dives down for a time. She then opens them and glides the rest of the way. Once her feet hit the ground, she lies down to allow me off. I climb off and she shakes out her feathers. She shifts. "Come follow me," she says as she walks off. I follow as I look around. I have been here once before; this place is absolutely beautiful, so full of life and nature.

We soon arrive at a big cave. "Come," Jaylen's mom says with a hand gesture. "Where are we?" The farther we go, the darker it gets. Soon, a small fireball appears to light the path. "We are in my sons' forge." After a lot of walking, we see light, and I am instantly surrounded by heat. "Ashore, lower the heat or you're going to break it!" I think it is Challet that yells that part. "Shut up, Jasper. I already did." Darn, I'm wrong. Jaylen's mom shakes her head.

Soon, I hear people running. "Mom!" they all say as they turn around. This is the time Jaylen decides to peek out from my pocket. They all look at her with wide eyes. She climbs out and lands on one of her brother's fingers. I think that it's Ashore. "That is correct," Jaylen says in the bond. Her brothers look over her like any other overprotective brothers would. "Why are you so tiny?" Ashore questions her, "And where is your brace... wait did you die?" Jasper asks like it is the most common thing in the world. "Yes, we still have the ashes." They all glare at me. "Come, Wolf Boy." I growl a little at the disrespect, but let it go because they are her brothers. This seems to have angered Jaylen, for she is now covered in flames. Ashore is now on the ground as he dodges the fireball.

"Ashore, don't disrespect Asland because, like it or not, he is the Fire Prince." Jasper yells out. It's hard to see him as the youngest brother out of the three. Ashore, the eldest, is very hot-headed, while Challet, the middle brother, is a bit too easy-going. The youngest brother, Jasper, is serious and takes control. I wonder just how old they are. They all look like they are in their twenties. "Ashore is four thousand, five hundred and seventy-eight years old, Challet is three thousand, five hundred and ninety, and Jasper is three thousand," Ruby answers, and my jaw drops. I'm scared to think how old she is. Ruby laughs, "For your information, I am one thousand and sixteen and Jaylen is only sixteen. If you want to know all our ages in phoenix standards then, Ashore is forty-five, Challet is thirty-five, Jasper is thirty, and I'm ten." This is so old in human years but so very young in phoenix years.

We follow her brothers deeper into the cave. They start running around the large room. Everything is neat and tidy. They gather a bunch of stuff; I don't even know what half of it is. "Don't worry, I don't either." Jaylen says. She is currently on my shoulder watching her brothers. I sit down leaning against the far wall. I watch until my eyes grow heavy. I wake up to someone kicking my foot. "Good evening, Asland," Challet says with an evil smirk on his face. "Wake up Ruby for us so we can put this on her." Fear shakes through my whole being. Jaylen hates being woken up.

However, I do really want to hold her in my arms. I slowly stand up, letting my muscles wake up. I gently pick her up from my shoulder so she doesn't fall. Then I gently shake her beak to wake her up. She opens her eyes and glares at me. I kiss her on the forehead and the glare instantly disappears. She lets out a purr-like sound and rubs her head against my nose. It tickles, and I laugh as I try to move her away. Her brothers look disappointed. Jaylen flips around so she is no longer on her back and stands still as Jasper puts the three bracelets on her and then backs up. I set her down and the shifting flame engulfs her. She instantly pulls me into a hug and kisses me. "I miss holding you," she whispers in my ear. I kiss her forehead. "So do I." I tighten my arms around her, never wanting to let go.

"Do you now have your original size or no?" I ask after a moment. "Nah, man. It'll take her at least a year to return to her original size," Challet says as he starts to clean up the forge. Jasper joins after giving Jaylen a hug. Jaylen tells me, "Mom is waiting outside for us. She will be taking us to our pack." I smile as she calls the pack ours. We say our goodbyes and head out. Jaylen's mom is in her phoenix form, asleep at the cave entrance. Jaylen gently pats her on the head, and her mom's eyes open. She yawns as she stretches. She lowers her body so Jaylen may hug it. "Are you ready to go?" Jaylen asks, turning to me. I nod and her mom lowers her neck so both of us may climb up. Jaylen is sitting in front of me and has the antennas. I just want to hold her, so that's what I do. We soon arrive at the pack land. Jaylen's mother slowly descends to the ground. I see my mom rushing out.

I get off, and she smiles a sad smile at me. I turn back to Jaylen, who mom hasn't noticed yet. I reach out my hand as I watch mom in the corner of my eyes. Jaylen grabs my hand and lets me help her down. Mom, now with tears in her eyes, looks to me, to Jaylen, and then to Jaylen's mom. "Dear, who's here?" I smile and gesture to Jaylen's mother. "Mom, meet Jaylen's mom." I pause as I try to remember her name. My face goes red with embarrassment. Bright light flashes for a second as she shifts. "I am Queen Powlistia Fire-rose, though please feel free to call me Listia. May I have the name of the one who raised such a great son?" I see mom flush as she smiles. "My name is Holly Noel Johnson. I am the luna of the Firestorm Pack until your daughter is ready to take over." Listia smiles as they both turn to us. "Goodbye for now." She kisses my forehead as well as Jaylen's. She shifts once more and flies away. My mom walks up to me and Jaylen. Mom hugs me and tightly hugs Jaylen. She whispers, barely loud enough for me to hear. "I'm glad you've returned to Asland's side." Mom lets go and steps back with tears pouring down her face.

ALPHA JACK

I get up from my desk and go into the hallway. It's now been a year since Jaylen's was reborn. She moved into the room across from mine. There's nothing really in it besides a bed and pictures of us to together on the walls and some pictures of her playing with the pups. It was so funny when she discovered the camera and phone. She begged me for one. Of course, I immediately went and got one for her. I smile at the memory, especially when she introduces it to her family. I'll do everything I can to keep the smile on her face.

Everything is not all bright and sunshine between us. We've got into many fights over the stupidest things that made Jaylen fly off to who knows where. After she comes back, she makes sure we discuss the issue and fix it. It has made us stronger as a couple. Nevertheless, her brothers still don't like me but I'm starting to think that it is all an act. I walk into my room and pull out a deep blue box from my nightstand. I open it to reveal the diamond ring. I've learned that phoenixes will not mate until married. I close the box with a smile. I don't mind at all.

I return the box into the drawer and close it. I walk back to my desk. I want the proposal to be as perfect as I can get it, based on the information given to me by her mother and what I learned myself. Jaylen loves beaches with black sand. Her favorite flowers are Easter Lilies. Her favorite colors are purple and blue. She loves amethysts and sapphires. I hear the elevator coming up and quickly hide all of the proposal ideas.

The elevator doors open, revealing mom and Lilly. I smile at them as Lilly comes running to me. "Aszy, when is J.J. going to become my sister?" My eyes widen at her question. Mom gives a sly smile. I give her a playful glare. "Soon, Lilly, soon." Mom eyes widen in shock and happiness. Lilly jumps up and down cheering. I shush her. "It's a surprise to Jaylen, so you can't say anything about it, okay?" Lilly nods, and I show her and mom my proposal plan, even though I know mom is the only one that's really looking at it. Lilly is just looking at the pretty pictures of the four beaches that I've found. The plan is to do it tomorrow. Jaylen returns from her princess duties today, and I can't wait for her to be in my arms.

Until that time, I will do my alpha duties as I wait for her. For the past week, she has called me every night, and she also texted me about her day and told me that she misses me and misses being Jaylen. Though we have the bond link, she is currently still obsessed with how the phone works. I suddenly feel pain shoot throughout my body from right shoulder. "Asland!" Mitchell bolts into my office, not even knocking. I would've yelled at him if he didn't look so panicked. The pain I'm currently in, well, it's actually Jaylen's pain. Mom took Lilly and left by the elevator. "What's wrong?" I ask with gritted teeth, both out loud and through the bond link with Jaylen. "This," he slams a piece of paper onto my desk. Something about the paper made him mad. I pick up the paper.

Dear Alpha Asland,

I just happened to have your beautiful Luna in my company. I say she is very feisty and her fire power is quite dangerous. Who knew phoenixes still existed? I was very shocked to see her alive when I shot her with an arrow. I wonder just how long she can scream until she dies and I get to do it all over again. Knowledge of how to kill a phoenix has been long lost. I'm excited to bring that knowledge to light once more.

Yours truly,
Alpha Jack

I growl as I tear the paper apart. How dare that rogue call himself an alpha? I'm going to kill him when I find him. I don't care that he is my uncle; he has crossed the line one too many times. "Every shifter must meet me in the training arena now!" I command through the mind-link with full force of an alpha. I even see Mitchell go to his knees under its weight. I enter the elevator with Mitchell behind me. He clicks the first floor button. I clench and unclench my fists. As I'm walking, I notice small flames start sparking at my fingertips then soon engulf my whole upper body. They burn off my shirt as they surround my arms and back. Mitchell lets out a whistle, getting the pack's attention.

"The rogue leader that has attacked us two years ago, as well as that killed Jaylen a year ago, has surfaced yet again. This time, he kidnapped her when she was returning to us." All of the pack members growl in anger. "Get ready, we are going to get our Luna back!" I yell, encouraging them, even though they don't need it. They are ready to fight to get their luna back. I need help to find her. I pull out my phone and call Jasper, since he's the one that is more reasonable than his brothers.

"Hello?" It sounds like he just woke up. "Jasper, I need help. Ruby was taken when she was coming back." I hear things falling then an alarm in the background. "Jasper, why did you sound the alarms?" I couldn't tell who asked this; I think it was Challet. "Ruby was taken!" Jasper yell. They also started calling her Ruby instead of her full name. The line is cut off and I put my phone back into my pocket. I turn back to my pack who look ready to kill. I'm about to speak when suddenly screeches of birds tear through the air.

We turn toward them to see the sky is full of fire shaped as birds, one leading the others in a V shape. The head must be Jaylen's mom, and the rest must be her flock. Soon, the phoenixes arrive at our pack. The queen lands first, followed by the others. All the phoenixes had men on their backs. There are at least a hundred phoenixes, though I know there are more back on the mountain. The king gets off and the queen shifts. "I hear Ruby was taken." I growl in anger as I nod. "Everyone you see here as of now is yours to command." I notice Ashore, Challet, and Jasper are also on phoenixes. Ashore is on a red-orange one with a pale gray and icy blue fox on his shoulder, Challet is on a red-yellowone, and Jasper is on an orange-red one. "We will also help," the king says as he walks up to me. I nod and turn to the others. It's time to form a plan.

Witches

It's now the third day. Her three brothers are exhausted and so are the other phoenixes. The phoenixes have been searching nonstop for three days for their princess. We have yet to find anything out about Jaylen's whereabouts. Right now, I'm heading to the Bloodstone Pack with Mitchell to see if they can help in the search. The only comfort I have is the buzzing feeling of the mate bond, but I can also feel her suffering, and it kills me each second that passes without me saving her from her torment.

I'm suddenly in so much pain that it makes me fall to the ground trembling. The mate bond has gone silent. Jaylen is dead. "Asland, what's wrong?" Mitchell asks through the mind-link, worry clear in his voice, not just for me but for his missing luna. I slowly get back up, my legs trembling in pain. I lift my head and let out a howl full of rage and sorrow. Mitchell and the others from my pack join in with rage and sorrow. I run faster toward the Bloodstone Pack. Through the pain, I feel a little comfort that they will now be unable to harm her. This buys us at least two weeks. "At least she will get two weeks of rest," Claude says sadly. His thoughts parallel my own thoughts; his emotions are also flowing through me. We must find her before she is reborn. Mitchell runs behind me. I wonder why it hurt so badly when she died this time? "Probably because she wasn't near us," Claude says, worried and sad.

It will take four days to get to Bloodstone. I could go to the neighboring packs, but I trust the Bloodstone Alpha. I've also become friends with his son who will be taking over in a year or two. "We'll find you Jaylen! Just wait for us!" I cry out with my whole being, hoping beyond hope that somehow, she will hear me and know she isn't alone. We soon get to the Bloodstone Pack. Surprisingly, they are already at the border in wolf form. The alpha changes. "We heard your howls; it was fate, and we knew it was you and that you need our help. I'll lend you ten warrior wolves. I wish I could do more." I shift and shake his hand in gratitude. "No, this is more than enough. You need your warriors to protect your pack. Thank you so much for your support." I turn and shift back to my fire wolf that my pack has named the hellhound. The ten instantly follow me and my beta as we return home.

It's been a month since Jaylen was taken and my pack is suffering. One, they don't have their luna, two, Claude is always on the surface, full of anger, and three, they lack proper sleep. There were many times where John and Mitchell had to hold me down before I harmed a pack member or the phoenixes. Jaylen also has yet to be reborn, which makes me feel both grateful and worried.

I hear knocking on my door. "What!" I growl out. I instantly stop when I see my mom. I take a deep breath as I sit up in bed, "Sorry, Mom." She gives me a sad smile. "It's okay, sweetheart." She walks up and hugs me. "Mom, she's going to be reborn soon, and we aren't even close to finding her. That rogue can harm her even more." She tightens her arms around me as I break down. Soon mom pulls away and wipes my tears from my face. "Go take a shower, and then there's someone here to see you. She says she might have the answer you're looking for." I nod and get up. I walk into the bathroom and take a shower. Once I'm done, I walk out and see myself in the mirror. I have very dark circles under my eyes and they are bloodshot. For the past two weeks, Claude has been searching for Jaylen's soul in the spirit realm, since it's a reflection of the mortal realm. Her soul will be near her ashes, but he has had no such luck finding her either.

At that thought, I hit the wall in frustration at my own uselessness. I leave my bathroom, which now has a hole in the wall. I get dressed in a plain red shirt and jeans. I enter my office to see mom glaring at an older lady next to a girl around my age. They both smell of starch and wood. Witches. Why are they here? "Is that your son? The alpha of this pack?" I growl at the older lady's tone toward my mother. "Shush it, mutt." I growl louder as Claude comes to the surface.

Claude may be more laid back than other alpha wolves, but he absolutely doesn't like being called a mutt. No wolf does. "Mother, you shouldn't disrespect the Firestorm Alpha. Especially if he is the alpha of my visions," the girl says. I turn to look toward the girl. The older lady lets out a sigh. "May we be alone with the alpha?" the girl asks my mother kindly. Mom turns and looks at me with worry. I nod for her to go; I'll be okay. Mom nods and leaves through the elevator.

"Sorry about my mother. She's angry because I dragged her all the way here because she wouldn't let me go alone." I look at her and her mother. They were covered in dirt and leaves. I sigh and mind link Jill. "Jill, come here for a moment." After a minute a soft knock breaks the silence. "Come in." The older lady glares at me. I ignore her as Jill nervously comes in- of course she's nervous! I've not been myself lately. "You wanted to see me, Alpha."

"Yes, take these two to the guest rooms on the Beta floor, let them have a shower and get them clean clothes, then bring them back to me after they eat something." All of them stare at me with wide eyes. They follow Jill out. I have twenty minutes to prepare myself for whatever reason the witches came to my pack. I lean back in my chair. "What do you think, Claude?" I ask as I close my eyes. "I'm not sure, I know that they are white witches, that there is no death on them, and that they are weaker than the witches that are with our uncle," he says, sounding just as tired as I am. The soft knock alerts me that the witches are back. I open my eyes and sit up once more. "Come in," Jill says as she opens the door for the two witches.

They look a lot better, and the older one looks happier. "Now that you guys had the chance to freshen up, please tell me why have you come here?" I try to be like my normal self toward the witches, hoping that they have good news for me. The girl gives a sad smile and pulls out a piece of paper. "Before we do, we need to make sure you are the one we must talk to." I nod, understanding where she is coming from. Witches' visions can be harmful to others if given to the wrong ears. She hands me the paper.

I look at it; it is a drawing of Jaylen holding another girl in a small room. A tear falls down my cheek as I see wounds all over Jaylen and the other girl.

I gently touch the picture. I don't like how it looks. If a witch with the gift of vision gives you a picture, it is real. "Yup, he's the one if he can see the picture." I look up at her, confused at what she means. "There's an enchantment on the drawing only the alpha of my visions may see. Not even my mother knows what it looks like." I nod and gesture toward the chairs in front of my desk. They both sit down; the girl suddenly starts to act nervous. I wonder why. "Alpha, may I have permission to enter your mind?" Oh, that's why. It's a big deal to ask an alpha to enter their mind; not even a pack member has access to that, only an alpha's mate does. "I promise not to look at anything; it's only to show you the visions," she quickly adds. Claude must've come to the surface.

I take a deep breath and nod my head, "but first tell me your names." The girl laughs, "Oh sorry. My name is Holly, and this is my mother Floria." I nod and watch them closely. Holly stands up and walks around my desk. I tense up at how close she gets. "Sorry but I must touch your forehead with mine." She explains once she stands next to me. I relax a little bit and turn to face her. I glance back at Floria. "What is Floria going to do?" I ask as nicely as I can under the circumstances.

"My mother is here to give me energy if I start to run out during the time I'm showing you the visions." I nod and look up at her. "Are you ready?" I nod. I hope I'll be able to find her. Holly pulls a chair up as close as she can get in front of me. She sits down and leans toward me, so I also lean down until both our foreheads touch. She starts chanting as she grabs my hands. I am about to pull away, but I instantly lose control over my body.

I am suddenly flying through the air over what appears to be an ocean and then over forests, and I stop in front of an old shack. I walk up to it. I go to turn the doorknob only to go through it. Confused, I try again and again as I go through it. I decide to just walk through the door. I soon see stairs going down. I walk down the stairs, memorizing all I can just in case. I reach the bottom and I see Jaylen laying down on her stomach with the girl cleaning the wounds on my mate's back. "Lorraine, please stop." The girl's name is Lorraine.

"Jaylen, why did you stop Mark from hurting me? I'm a witch, I can take the pain." Jaylen lets out a short laugh before hissing in pain. "I believe you can take the pain but you are no witch." Lorraine looks at Jaylen. "What do you mean? I have fire and water magic, which they somehow blocked at the moment." Jaylen slowly pushes herself off the ground. She continues to hiss in pain until she is fully sitting up. "Witches can have two elements but they can't be the opposite of each other. You are a half phoenix and half human with a water spirit's blessing. Either you got it when you were born or it was your mom, and the reason you can't use magic is because there's a furbla herb that blocks phoenix powers and spirit connection."

"Wait, if that's true, then can I turn into a bird too." Jaylen shakes her head. "No, you got your blood from a male phoenix. They don't carry the shifting trait. There is a way to get you a phoenix spirit, but you must get the queen phoenix's blessing." The door bursts open. "Well, well, well. Looks like you two made friends." Jaylen instantly hugs Lorraine. It was just like the drawing. "I won't let you hurt her." Jaylen is pulled away by her hair.

The man then stabs her in the heart. He then throws her away from him. Jaylen is slowly lit on fire by the golden flames. It is very different from before. Jaylen is soon just a pile of ashes. Lorraine cries out and tries to get to Jaylen's ashes. Everything dissolves into nothing. I open my eyes and see Holly breathing very heavy, and she is sweating. I pull back and mind-link Jill to come to the office. She soon knocks on the door. "Come in." She enters, and she still looks extremely nervous. "Jill, take Holly and Floria back to the guest rooms they used before and let them sleep." She nods and leads them away. So that is how she died. I must find her quickly before they hurt her or Lorraine again.

Norway

I get up from my desk and walk to Jaylen's room. I slowly turn the doorknob and push the door open. I'm greeted by the pictures she took and also the pictures the pack has given her. Mom even gave her some of me as a pup. I pick up her favorite picture off her nightstand. It is a picture my mom took of me asleep on the couch with a sleeping Jaylen in my arms. I begged Mom to delete it but Jaylen begged to have a copy. She won of course; she always gets anything that puts a smile on her face, though she rarely ever asks and is always considerate to others no matter what.

Everyone loves their luna, for she listens to them with almost all of her attention. She does get distracted by animals and children, but everyone grew to love that about her. She's extremely protective of the pack, of nature, and, most of all, of me. It's a little weird at times but she doesn't get in my way and she does not make me feel inferior. She allows me to protect her from males and from as much pain as I can, though I've not been doing a good job on either of those things. I put the picture back onto her nightstand next to her alarm clock. It's two in the morning, just how long did that vision take? Oh well, I need to eat something. I walk to the end of the room and close the door when I exit. I head to the kitchen, thinking of what to make. I look into my fridge. A meat sandwich it is. I gather the stuff and put it together. I go to take a bite when I feel a faint buzzing wrap around my heart. Tears reach my eyes; she's alive again.

Suddenly, my kitchen doors bursts open. "I know where she is!" I growl at Holly for entering my private floor without permission but instantly stop once her words register. "Where is she?" I stand up so fast it makes me dizzy. "She's in Bymarka forest in Norway." My eyes widen. "Norway! How on earth did they get to Norway?!" I yell. No wonder we can't find a trace of her. Holly seems unfazed by my anger and continues. "I saw a Kelpie near the hut where the luna and girl are."

"Kelpie! Those sea horseman are stupid." Holly nods. Kelpies can teleport to any body of water with anything they want, although they normally stay to themselves and hate the land. How on earth are we going to get to Bymarka, Norway from Bernheim, Kentucky? Norway is halfway across the world. Wait a second, I know exactly the people I need. I pull out my phone and call Ashore. I don't care that it's three in the morning. "What?!" Ashore yells in anger. "I know where Ruby is." Instantly I hear Ashore yelling at his brothers to come to their parents' room. I hear a door opening. "Ashore, what on earth are you doing?" The king asks, sounding scared and annoyed. "What's with all your yelling?"

"Asland, repeat what you said." He must've put me on speaker. "I found out where Ruby is being held." I move my phone away from my ear knowing what is about to happen. "WHERE?!" They all yell into the phone. "In Bymarka, Norway." I again move my phone away. One, two, three, "NORWAY! What's she doing in Norway?!" I roll my eyes, "one, it wasn't her choice, and two, how fast can we get there?"

I hear laughing, why are they laughing? "It'll take us a day at most. Two if we have more than two people on us." The queen answers, "Well then, I'll get everyone ready for the flight." With this, I hang up. "Alpha, once we get our luna back, can I ask for a favor?" I turn and face Holly. "Holly, once I have Jaylen you can ask for anything in my power to give." She smiles and leaves. "Everyone over sixteen, meet me out in the training field." I mind-link everyone as I head to my elevator. It's time to bring Jaylen home.

I get to the field where everyone is waiting. They all look like they are half-dead. "I have good news and bad news. The good news is that I know where your luna is." Everyone cheers and is instantly full of energy and hope. "The bad news is that she's in Norway." They all growl. "The other good news is that the phoenixes are going to fly us there, and we'll be there within a day."

Right as I finish talking, many cries of the phoenixes pierce the air. They all land in the clearing; there are thousands of them. there are also dragons and griffins. Some have mates on their backs and some don't. "Everyone, go to a phoenix that doesn't have a person on their back. Fire Prince, you're with me," a girl says, walking up and bowing at me.

"Who are you?" I ask. She looks up and smiles. "My name is Comadollia. You can call me Dollia or Grandma." Grandma? She looks like she's eighteen. She laughs, "I'm a phoenix dear. I stopped aging when I had Powlistia." This means she's Jaylen's grandma. Dollia shifts into a pure red phoenix. I thought they always had a second color. She also doesn't have the antennas like Jaylen and the others do. I wonder why? Dollia lays down and I get on. "Everyone ready?" I ask with a shout. I get yelling and cheers as answers back. "Let's go!" All the phoenixes, dragons, and griffins fly off.

As we are flying, my eyes start to get very heavy. I allow sleep to take me for I need all the rest I can to save Jaylen and that girl. I wake up when Dollia lands. The sun is now down and stars shine in the night sky. Everyone in my pack and the Bloodstone Pack shifts into wolves and falls asleep. I join them, for we need all the rest we can get. In the morning, three phoenixes scout out the place by air. They say that there are over a thousand rogues surrounding the hut. They say that the best time to strike will be when Jaylen turns back into a human. That will be in six days. That's plenty of time to rest and plan for the war.

War in a Storm

It's now the sixth day that we've been in Norway. Everyone is now fully recovered and ready for war to get our Luna back. Norway has a charm about it, but I can't wait to get Jaylen back home. Right now, we're waiting for Ashore and May's signal to attack. Everyone is watching the sky for it. There it is- the fire rose.

"Let's go!" I yell, shifting into my hellhound. "Let's get our mate back," Claude growls and is ready to kill. All the phoenix burst into flames and fly off with the dragons and griffins. All the wolves shift and run behind me. We burst out of the forest, but the rogues are ready to fight us. They just aren't prepared for dragons, griffins, and phoenixes. Fire is everywhere and griffins are taking wolves high in the air and dropping them. Our wolves are painted with a magic gold stripe from their nose down their backs that protects them from fire for three days, also, the griffins do not to take them to the sky for flying lessons. It's not hard to find me at all, especially when I'm in berserk mode.

Suddenly, a lightning storm appears and rain comes out of nowhere. There weren't even clouds in the sky when we started, but now they rain is pouring on us. To make things even weirder, the lightning strikes are only hitting the rogues and the hut. Everyone freezes, watching the rogues get hit over and over again. They don't get any time to heal. "Asland, let's head to the hut while this freak storm has the rogues districted," Mitchell mind-links me. I nod and run straight toward the hut. Mitchell is soon behind me.

Once in the hut, Mitchell starts growling like crazy. We both shift since our wolves are too big to go down the stairs. "Mitch, are you okay?" Mitchell turns to me, and I see that his wolf is in control. "Zeke, what's wrong?" Zeke turns back to the stairs. "My mate is down there with the luna. She is crying and in pain." I nod; he's worried. "Then what are we waiting for? Let's go get our girls." We rush down the stairs two at a time. We soon reach the bottom of the floor with an empty room. I can smell that Jaylen was here, but where is she now?

Zeke starts sniffing everywhere and finds something I don't want to be there. He finds a body of water. I pull out my phone and call Holly. "Can you find her?" I don't wait for her to say hello. "YES!" she yells happily, "Oh sorry. The water spirits are holding the Kelpie back. They are near the lake that is east of us." Zeke and I race out of the hut. We shift and head east toward the lake. I wonder why the water spirits are helping. They are like the Kelpie; they stay close to the water but once in a while, they do give a human a water blessing. This allows them to control water or even the weather, depending on how strong the spirit is that gives the blessing.

Wait, can the rogues have a blessed child? The water spirits are very protective of their blessed children. Lorraine! In the vision, Lorraine said that she can control water. She is the blessed child and also a half phoenix, so she's very powerful. Wait, there were only two female scents in that room. Could Lorraine be my beta female? Now, this gives me even more reason to get them back home and safe.

We reach the lake and see four giant balls of water. A water spirit appears in front of me. "May I inquire as to why has thou comest here?" The water spirits aren't any bigger than my hellhound's nose., but you are unable kill them since they don't have a physical body. If you destroy the item they're attached to, then they will disappear, and the item can literally be anything in the freaking ocean. I shift to answer the spirit. The water spirit floats up to my eye level. "I'm looking for my mate. A witch named Holly told me that she is here."

"We have your mate and your beta's mate. You must find the bubble that has your mate. If you choose the right one, you shall receive your mate." With this, the water spirit drops to the ground, making a tiny puddle. Water spirits love to play tricks, but they never lie. I close my eyes and follow where the mate pull takes me. Soon, I hear the sound of water above me.

I open my eyes just as the bubble pops, and Jaylen drops into my arms. "It looks like both of thou have found thy mates. Thou alpha of wolves and phoenixes, thy mate had something that broke thy mind. She shall not be herself until thy fixes herself. Thy beta protects our blessed child. She is the last one, and a powerful one at that. If thou cannot protect our blessed child, we shall take her away from thou."

Zeke growls at the threat of taking his mate away. Never threaten to take someone's mate away; it always ends badly. "Zeke, let's get them home." Zeke stops growling and nods toward me. I turn and run back to the others with Jaylen in my arm. She looks like she's in so much pain. I wish I could take it all away. I lean close to her and whisper, "I'm so sorry my love. I wish this had never happened to you. I never want you in pain or away from my side." Tears rolls down her cheeks, though her eyes never open. "Asland," she whimpers. I can feel the sadness within her, though I don't know the cause.

"They're back, and they have the luna and the girl!" I hear someone yelling to the others. We enter into our camp. "Is everyone ready to go home?" I ask as I enter the camp, and everyone cheers. I hop onto Dollia with Jaylen in my arms. I soon fall asleep once again, but this time it is with Jaylen safe in my arms. I'm awakened by a scream. I look down and see a very frightened Jaylen. It hurts to see nothing but fear is in those beautiful blue eyes that were once filled with life and love. However, that isn't what hurt the most- it is what she says, "Who are you and where is my mate?"

Home Safe But Not Sound

When we get home, Jaylen quickly gets away from me. She sees that everyone in her flock is here. First, her face is full of confusion and then full of fear. "Jaylen, what's wrong?" Her eyes start to tear up. "Ruby. She's gone. I cannot feel her." This isn't good. Just what has my uncle done to my mate? "Sweetheart, are you okay?" her mom asks as she starts to walk over. Jaylen starts to shake in fear. I instinctively wrap my arms around her. "No! Let go of me. Only my mate may touch me!" She yells. I'm glad she will only let her mate touch her, but she doesn't realize that I am her mate. "I am your mate, Jaylen." I tried to stay calm because of what she just went through. So, this is what the water spirit was talking about.

"No, you're lying." She tries her hardest to get out of my arms as I try my hardest not to hurt her by holding on too tight. "Sweetheart, what he says is true; he is your mate." Jaylen turns to her mom. "Then how come I don't remember him? I don't even know his name or species." Claude whimpers at the realization that forgot everything about us. "He's a werewolf, well, not exactly, but close enough and he's name is..." I shake my head no. I want her to remember my name herself. "You can call him Alpha Johnson until you remember his name."

"Fine, Alpha Johnson, please let go of me." I really dislike her using my title and last name. She is my luna, my equal, and my world. I take a deep breath and let go of her. She walks away from me toward her family. "Let's go home now." I want to yell that she is home, but I hold my tongue. "Sweetheart, you are home." Jaylen turns and looks at the pack house. "I don't remember us moving down the mountain." Her mom shakes her head. "Sweetie, you moved in with your mate a year ago." Jaylen looks shocked and instantly turns red.

I realize something. Her mom never called her sweetheart; it was always Rubeastia that did this. She just barely started calling her Ruby, but not once did she ever call her sweetheart. Her mom puts her hand on Jaylen's forehead. "I see, Ruby must've left with the memories of your mate when you got an injection." Jaylen's eyes widen and so do mine. They already know about Jaylen. "Sweetheart, I know this is going to be hard without Ruby but you must stay with Alpha Johnson. He will do everything in his power to help you." Tears enter Jaylen's eyes. "Mom, do I really need to be here?" Everyone in the flock nods. "Yes, sweetie." She hugs her, "Whether you have Ruby or not, you will always be my daughter." Jaylen is fully crying now.

Jill takes Jaylen by the shoulders. "Alpha, I'll take Luna to her room. Do I have permission to enter your floor?" I nod, "Yeah use the elevator and make sure she's comfortable." Jill nods as she walks away with Jaylen. "Asland, be patient. Ruby will return to her with her memories of you. I have a feeling that she had a reason." Her mom pats my shoulder then pulls me into a hug. "They are both my daughters, so I know that they are strong and as their mate, you are also strong so all of you will get through this." With that, she shifts and flies away with her husband. I mind-link all pack members. "From this day on, I'm Alpha Johnson until our luna says my name." Everyone says, "Yes Alpha." I walk toward the pack house and meet with everyone in my pack to see how they are doing. Everyone is very happy to have their luna back, and they hope that she gets her memories back soon. After meeting everyone, it is close to nine o'clock. I head up to my floor. I walk out of my elevator into my office. I walk to my desk and decide to do some paperwork.

I'm awoken by a gentle shake. I open my eyes only to meet bright blue ones. My head lightens, and I smile softly. "I'm sorry, Alpha Johnson. I used your kitchen to make breakfast, saw you sleeping here, and thought that you might want to eat something." My smile grows at her words. I sit up and rub my face with a sigh. I am so happy to her voice again. "Thank you, and don't worry, you have all access to everything in this house, especially this floor." She nods and heads out of the office. I notice a blanket on one of my shoulders and look at the time. It is nine o'clock. I get up and stretch out my muscles. Sleeping at my desk is awful. I remember Jaylen always scolded me that it would hurt my back later on in life.

I walk into the kitchen and see her sitting, looking at a picture. As I walk up, I start to see the picture more clearly. It is the picture of me and her sleeping on the couch. "I guess you really are my mate. I would never do anything like this with anyone but my mate. So why don't I remember you?" She starts to cry, and I sit down next to her and pull her into a hug. "Shh, it's okay. Ruby will be back with your memories. I'm not sure why she left with them, but she had a reason and she will be back."

She looks at me and nods, "Will you please tell me your name? It's awful calling you Alpha when you are my mate." I shake my head no. "Sorry, I can't do that. That's what will tell me you have your memories back, and the pack will know that you are healed." She nods and gets up. She grabs the two plates. "Here, can you at least answer some of my questions?" I shrug my shoulders, "Sure, why not?" She smiles and asks, "Okay first, off how did we meet?" I smile at the memory of this. "There's no easy way to say this; you killed me." She stares at me like I grew two heads. "That's impossible. If you were to die. . ." I interrupt her. "…You'd be dead too. I know; however, when Ruby used the rebirth flame, the flame within me revived me as well as you. Remember when your mom said that I was a werewolf then said I was not exactly a werewolf?" Jaylen looks at me with wide eyes. "I'm now a fire wolf, and my pack calls me a hellhound." She shakes her head, "That's not possible." I can see she wants to leave, so I quickly change the subject. She mainly quizzes me, to see how much I know about her, which is a lot. She's a very open book if she wants to be. I don't tell her everything about us, although it is still easy to talk to her even if she doesn't remember me.

THIRD MONTH

It's now the third month of me being in this house. The witch that helped the alpha rescue me is now a permanent part of the pack, as she requested. I'm currently sitting on what is supposedly my bed, staring at a photo of me and Alpha Johnson. In fact, there are so many pictures of him in this room. I walk to the wall with the most pictures. In the center of them is the alpha, and he is smiling. The alpha is a very handsome man. "Why can I not remember you?" I ask as I gently touch the photo. I jump at the sound of a knock. I turn and see the luna, my mate's mother. Ugh, it kills me not to know his name, and no one is telling me it either. "Hello, dear." I nod to her. For the past few weeks I have acted like I look in the pictures, and it feels so familiar to me.

"Would you like to come on a walk with me?" she asks. She has been the most helpful to me with my memory problems. Even though Alpha Johnson helps a lot with my memory problems, I no longer ask him to help since it hurts me so badly to see the pain in his eyes. Even if he tries to hide it, I know that me not remembering him hurts him. I look at Luna, and she smiles at me. "Yes, let's go for a walk." I get up and gently set the framed photo of me on the Alpha on the nightstand. "Oh, I remember taking that one Ja-. . .Alpha Johnson told me to delete it multiple times, but you asked him to have it one time, and he smiled and gave in." I notice that she pauses after saying this, as I quickly act like I did not notice and laugh. Could this be a clue to his name?

After the small walk, it's late and my body is tired. I bid the luna goodnight and close my door. I walk to the window and stare up at the night sky. I turn around with a yawn. I climb into the covers and quickly fall asleep.

I see Alpha Johnson standing against the moonlight. He reaches out his right hand. I smile as I grab it. He pulls me up easily into his arms. He doesn't let go of my hand as he wraps his left arm around my wrist. "I didn't think my mate would fall out of the sky like a meteor," he whispers in my ear, sending a chill down my spine. I still don't recall his name. Suddenly, he disappears into the night. I'm now at a table with a plate of food in front of me. I take a bite. "Yum, this is heavenly. You are now my personal chef." I smile at Alpha Johnson. "Oh, and here I thought I was your mate," he says with mock hurt. This time I teasingly give him a smile. "You are, and you belong only to me," I say as I kiss Alpha's cheek. "And you belong only to me," he says, as he grabs my chin and kisses me. I freeze in shock at first, but then I kiss him back. I feel so happy, then the feeling dissolves into nothing. What is happening?

I'm now in a very familiar place; it's my cave with the nest. I turn toward the mirror but instead of seeing my reflection, I see the alpha untying his wet shirt with ashes. He looks a little surprised to see them still dry. "See I'm still here; there is still life in those ashes!" I hear my voice yet again as well as tears in my eyes. I feel as though he will not hear me. I watch as he falls to his knees. "Why did you jump in front of me?" His voice sounds so broken. My heart shatters at his pain though I don't know why.

Then the scene in the mirror changes. I see Alpha is currently eating with his mom, when Mitchell bursts in. "We. Found. The. Rogue. Pack. And. One. Of. Them. Had. A. Very. Bad. Burn. On. His. Arm." Mitchell says after every breath. My heart is suddenly filled with panic at his words. Yet again, I'm not sure why I feel this way. I then feel rage and I somehow know that it's from the faceless man and his need for revenge. "Don't do it!" I yell pounding against the mirrored wall. He runs out of the kitchen and down the stairs. I feel tears pouring down my cheek and heart aching. "Please Asland, don't do this!" I cry out with all of my strength, as I know that he has no ties to life. "ASLAND!" I yell with all of my strength.

I quickly sit up and look around. I'm in my room in the alpha's floor. What a weird dream. I rub the sleep out of my eyes, only to find my face wet. Did I cry in my sleep? I try to remember the dream but nothing comes to mind. I feel as if it was very important. Why can't I remember it? My stomach growls. I'll think about more after I eat. I quickly take a shower, and I decide to wear clothes today. I grab a beautiful white turtleneck shirt with a lavender scarf and blue skinny jeans. I walk to the kitchen and see Alpha cooking. "Jaylen, I made some breakfast. Come eat." Tears start to fall from my eyes, even though he has yet to turn around. I cover my mouth as the dream comes back to me. "I'm back! Did you miss me?" Ruby chirps inside my head. 'Sorry, it took a while to get all the toxins out of your bloodstream. I returned as soon as possible. It must've hurt a lot not to remember him, didn't it?' she says softly.

"I'm just glad that you are back with our memories, too." "Jaylen are you okay?" asks Asland, who must have felt my sudden burst of emotions. I stop my tears. He looks panicked, like he is fighting the urge to run up and hug me. I know that without my memories, I kept a distance between us. I smile at him. He smiles back hesitantly. "Come, let's eat," he says as he sets two plates down. I sit and start eating. After I finish, I stand up and kiss his cheek. His body tenses, and I say, "Thanks for breakfast, Asland, I'll wash the dishes." I pick up his plate and mine. I walk away to the kitchen sink and put the dishes in it. I turn and see Asland standing by the table, staring at me.

"Jaylen, what did you just say?" I knew what he wanted to hear, but I just had to mess with him a little. "Thanks for breakfast?" I ask innocently, he frowns slightly. "No after that." I pretend to think about it. "I'll wash the dishes?" This time he frowns deeper, and I see doubt forming in his beautiful green eyes. "No, before that," he says so softly that I can barely hear him; he is now looking at the floor. He looks so defeated. "Asland, an alpha should never lower his head. You are my mate, so hold your head up high." His head shoots straight up, and his eyes are wide. I smile at him and let Ruby have control. "Hello, love." I see a tear fall from his eyes as he smiles just as wide as I did. "You're back with us." Ruby nods, "Me and all of the memories," she says to both to me and Asland. I feel the tears coming, "Why exactly did you leave?" Asland asks he sits back down. Ruby walks over and sits on his lap. Asland hugs our waist as we rest our head on his chest. "They injected us with a witch poison meant to permanently sever the bond between mates. I gathered as much of the bond and memories that I could within me and temporarily cut the tie to me and Jaylen until the toxins were completely out of her bloodstream."

Story of Captivity

"You should also see my memory." Jaylen sits down in front of me and touches her forehead with mine. Instantly, my mind connects with hers. "Jaylen, I have a bad feeling. I think we should stay here for one more day." Her emotions mirror my own. She wants to be back with Asland as much as I do, but I can't shake the feeling that if we go now then we won't see him for a long time. "Ruby, it'll be alright, we've been away from him for a week before," I tell Ruby. "I just want to hold him so much," she says and I sigh. She can be such a child, though I have to admit that does sound amazing. "Come on, let's go." She runs out and calls the shifting flames. I try to ignore my growing concern as we fly off to see our lovely mate.

The wind feels great in our feathers while we close the distance between us and our mate. As we near the pack, we start to descend. Suddenly, pain surges throughout our body, starting at our chest. "What's happening?" Jaylen starts to panic as we fall out of the sky. "I don't know." We crash to the ground and pain shoots through our right wing. I think it might be broken. "Jaylen, can you shift?" She calls onto the sifting flames, and we shift into our human body and two spirits. We force ourselves to sit against the trees.

"Well, look who we have here," a deep voice says. The smell of something rotten comes closer. "I believe I shot you when you decided to jump in front of that mutt of an alpha." A weak flame surrounds our body from his disrespect of our mate. "Oh, you're a phoenix. They say that phoenixes rise from their ashes." The fire goes out; I can't stay awake any longer. "Looks like it's taking effect." What did he put in us? I feel Jaylen's consciousness becoming faint. I faintly feel another phoenix. I take over our body to open our eyes. I see a girl who's surrounded by the phoenix's light. "Hello, I'm Lorraine," the girl says. I stand up and walk up to her. Her light brightens, acknowledging me. However, I can feel that she doesn't have a phoenix within her. She's shaking. Am I frightening her? I feel Jaylen stir and allow her to take control. "Hello, sorry about Ruby. She's a bit intimidating, but she's very sweet once you get through all of her walls. I'm Jaylen by the way." Lorraine looks very confused. "What are you?"

Jaylen smiles, but before she can answer, the door bursts open, revealing a man covered in scars. Lorraine whimpers and tries to disappear in the corner. She's afraid of this man. I take over and stand my ground. "Get on your knees, girl." I refuse. I'm the daughter of the phoenix queen. I will never lower myself to one who is below me. I'm about to say just this, but Jaylan speaks firs,. "I will not." The man gives us an evil smile and pulls out a whip. Of course, the first thing that he will do is hurt us. I take the pain, not letting Jaylen feel it.

I notice that my connection with Jaylen is slowly fading. There must be furbla herbs around here. "Jaylen, be careful. There must be furbla herbs around here. Soon, I won't be able to talk to you." I feel that Jaylen didn't like that thought. "Jaylen, why did you do that?" Lorraine crawls over to us as we lay on our stomach. Lorraine starts to clean our back with water. Where did she get water? I don't see anywhere that you can get it.

"What are you? I'm a witch. I can control fire and water, though I can't use my fire." I laugh; of course it's a water spirit blessing. I take over and continue to laugh, which now hurts since it's not in my head anymore. I hiss in pain as I try to sit up. "Witches can have two of the elements, but they can't be the opposite of each other. You are a half phoenix and half human with a water spirit blessing. Either you got it when you were born or your mom, and the reason you can't use the magic of the phoenixes is because there's an furbla herb that blocks phoenix powers and spirit connection."

"Wait, if that's true, then can I turn into a bird too." I shake my head, "No, you got your blood from a male phoenix. They don't carry the shifting trait, though there is a way to get you a phoenix spirit, but you must first get the Queen Phoenix's blessing." The door bursts open. "Well, well, well. Looks like you two made friends." My phoenix instincts kick in, and I instantly hug Lorraine. "I won't let you hurt her." I'm pulled away by my hair. I try to get him to let go of my hair but the whip stops me. This is continued and repeated daily. Until one day when Lorraine has enough. She yells at Mark and attacks him with water. A man then races in, and I am held and stabbed in the heart. I know Jaylen will have most of the pain since our connection is very faint. I watch as Jaylen enters the spirit world. "What's the plan when we go back?" She sits in the grass. "We need to find a way to get ahold of Asland."

"Man, it's too bad we can't contact anyone spiritually unless we're linked or mated." My eyes widen, of course! Why didn't I think of that? Witches are able to communicate with spirits. "I've got an idea. I'll be back." I fly off, following the pull of Claude. I feel closer as I fly over an ocean. Soon, I feel the connection of Jaylen straining. I land and that's when I see a witch's soul. It's a very young witch, but she will do. I give the soul all of the information I know and tell her who to give it to. I quickly fly back to Jaylen. She smiles at me. "I'm not sure if it'll work, but I hope so. For now, just sleep and gain strength. We're going to need it." She nods and goes to sleep until it'll be time for her to return. I also go to sleep to gain strength. Jaylen wakes up and returns while I continue to gather strength for her. I suddenly feel a strong amount of fear coming from the now very faint tie between us. I decide to enter her mind to see what has gotten her so scared.

"So, apparently Asland has decided to finally pay a visit. So now I have to give you one final gift." He pulls out a needle syringe. "Don't worry, all this will do is kill every memory of that useless mutt, oh and that annoying thing that's a mate bond." NO! I quickly gather all her memories on the bond within me and fully cut the link between us. The pain of losing her spirit hurts. I watch her body as the liquid enters her changing her soul from white to blue. I gather strength as I continue to watch her. I see Claude searching for me, but as long as I'm not connected to a body, no one can feel or see me. Soon, I start to see her soul return to white. When her soul is once again pure white, I reconnect our souls, returning to the world and bringing her memories of Asland with me.

IT'S PAST TIME

I wake up to the sun shining in my eyes. "Good morning, Asland." I turn and see Jaylen eating a chocolate bar. "Hey, where's mine?" I joke, only for a chocolate bar to come flying toward my head. I catch it and give her a warm smile. A Milky Way- my favorite. I open it and take a bite. "Lorraine wants to go to the mall. She asked if I'll like to go. I said I'll ask you since I haven't really been able to be with you for a long time." I smile at her and a plan starts forming in my head. "That's perfect. Let's do it!" Claude cheers and howls in delight.

"Sure, go ahead. I have a few calls to make and a few people to meet." She looks at me with a hint of suspicion since I called off most of my meetings for a few weeks to help her. She seems to let it go. I have no calls to the others packs, but I am not lying. I do have calls to make to her family, and then I have members of my pack I need to meet. She walks up and gives me a kiss on the cheek. "See you later, then." I nod and she gives me a quick hug and walks away. I grab her arm and pull her into a kiss. I pull back and whisper in her ear, "I love you." She pushes away with tears in her eyes. "I love you, too," she says with a smile. Girls are so confusing. How can you cry and smile at the same time? I pull her into a hug. "Okay, off you go before Lorraine lights the place on fire."

"Haha, very funny Alpha. I'm stealing Luna for the day." I nod as Lorraine appears in my mate's room. I grab my wallet and hand Jaylen my card. Jaylen

137

kisses me and runs off with Lorraine. I mind-link Lorraine. "Oh, and Lorraine, you might want to take Jaylen to the dress shop since I'm proposing tonight but don't say anything." I hear a loud squeal that can only be Lorraine. Just to be funny, I mind-link Jaylen. "Jaylen, is everything okay? I heard an unearthly scream?" Jaylen laughs, "That was just Lorraine. Mitchell must've told her she has unlimited use of his credit card or something." Or something. I was actually the cause of the squeal. "Oh, okay have fun."

I pull out my phone to start the plan. I look through the contacts and see Dollia's number. All the phoenixes have phones now, but they aren't made by humans; they make them on their own. I don't know how they figured out how to make one, let alone a thousand or so of them. "Hello?" Dollia's voice answers the phone. "Hey, Dollia, I need a favor." I walk to my office to start gathering up the stuff I need. "Oh, of course, ask away." I open a drawer and pull out the box. "I need a ride to the mountain. It's time I ask for Jaylen's hand." I hear a squeal and then running. "I'm on my way."

Okay. One thing done, many more to go. I mind-link Mitchell to come to my office. He is there in a flash. "Yo 'Land, wanted to see me?" I roll my eyes and hand him a pile of papers. He stares at them in horror; he hates paperwork. "They're not paperwork. They're a blueprint." Mitchell furrows his eyebrows in confusion. He quickly scans the blueprints and smiles. "Well, it's about time. No wonder Lorraine squealed this morning." He pats the papers, "Bro, consider this done."

"Thanks," I say, as I hear the call of an eagle. "Well, that's my ride to go ask Jaylen's family for their blessing." Mitchell pats my back. "Dude, you already have it." I roll my eyes and walk into the elevator. Once the door opens on the first floor, I run outside and greet Dollia. She lowers her neck to allow me on the elevator. Once on the elevator, Dollia flies off toward the mountain. As we fly there, I start to think of a way to ask. We arrive sooner than I thought we would. "Dollia, did you fly faster on purpose?" She gives a bird-like laugh as she lowers her neck. I get off of her and head to the castle. Dollia flies off to who knows where. Right as I step into the doors, I'm dragged off by five phoenixes. I'm put into a room, and they give me a white military looking uniform with gold trim and rope. I put it on, and as I finish putting the cape on the phoenixes come in. "They are ready for you, Fire Prince." I nod, "The only thing I need is a sword and I'll really look like an olden day prince." They smile and say, "There is an actual sword that goes with it. We can get it if you want."

You have got to be kidding me. Jaylen told me that phoenixes love the medieval times. I just didn't know it is this extreme. "No, thanks," I say, and I'm about to walk out. "Come on, aren't you curious about what it could look like?" Claude smirks, knowing tha I didn't want to carry the sword. I knew if they bring it, I'll have to carry it with me. "Never mind. I'd like to see it," I tell them. They cheer and run of to get the sword.

They return with a white and gold sheathed sword with a gold handle. I pick it up and go to open it but it won't budge. "You won't be able to open it until the marriage ceremony is finished." Oh, okay, so it's a useless sword for now. I hand them back the sword and head off to take care of the main reason why I'm here. I enter the throne room. Instantly I hear, "Finally, it's about time." I give the queen a warm smile at her outburst. Everyone in the room including Jaylen's brothers smile back at me. Everyone gives me their blessing.

My One and Only

I walk out of the castle and every phoenix cheers. How did they know? Did the queen tell them? "It's your outfit. You're wearing the Fire Prince uniform, so they know you are going to propose or already have," Jasper says next to me. I look at the white and gold uniform and smile. "Well, at least I don't have to tell them." Jasper laughs, "Nope. They can all see their prince." We laugh until Dollia lands in front of us. She shifts and smiles at me. "Need a ride back?" She smiles. I still can't get over the fact that she's way older than eighteen.

"Yes, can you take me to this location?" I hand her a piece of paper. "Certainly, hop on." She hands me the paper and shifts back into a phoenix. I get on, and she flies away. The flight is calming and peaceful. Soon, my days will be full of joy, laughter, some hardships, and, most of all, love. We land in the black sand of Maui. I climb off of Dollia, and she flies away. I walk along the seashore, the waves barely reaching my shoes. Soon, I see the sapphires and candles leading to the area I'm looking for. Mitchell will be bringing Jaylen to the other end of the sapphires. She will follow them to me where I'll then go to my knee and propose. "Alpha, we just landed. We are heading into the car now," Mitchell links me.

I smile at the blue box in my hand. Suddenly, I feel pure joy pouring through me. I knew Jaylen is nearby. "We just reached the path. Jaylen is already crying," Mitchell says in a teasing manner. "We all know why she's crying. I'm sending her off." I stand up straighter with my hands behind my back and a smile on my face. Soon, Jaylen appears in a breathtaking blue dress. Her feathers beside the antennas are gone. She is smiling with tears in her eyes. Right as she sees me, her hands goes up to her face.

Once she is standing in front of me, I drop to one knee and pull out the ring. "Jaylen Ruby Fire-Rose, you've brought me much joy and strength when I needed it. You've been by my side for the past three years. Even though we have had hardships, they made us stronger and wiser. You have given me so much since we met. I've brought you here to ask you, will you do me the honor of being your husband and the father of your future children?" I open the box, revealing the ring. Tears pour down her cheeks. She lowers her hands revealing a smile, "Yes. What took you so long to ask me?"

I laugh at her teasing and slide the ring onto her left hand. I stand up and kiss her. I then pick her up and spin joyfully. We both laugh and kiss again. "I love you, Jay." She gives me a loving look. "As I love you, Asland." We walk barefoot in the water, hand in hand. I pull her into my arms and watch the sunset as the waves hit our feet. I kiss her ringed hand. We walk to the car, I drive to the airport, and we fly back to the pack. Jaylen falls asleep in my arms on the plane.

It is now the big day. Jaylen has been stressed out for the past four months with planning the wedding. Of course, I did as much as I could do while doing my alpha duties. My mom and Jaylen's mom mainly helped her. I helped with the cake tasting and the food, but everything else is just out of my realm of expertise. I'm now back in the Fire Prince uniform in front of the altar, but this time, the sword is on me. Every wolf of my pack, plus all of the members of the phoenix, dragon, griffin, witch, and humans who are in the phoenix clans are here sitting, waiting for Jaylen to arrive. Soon the music starts and out of the forest comes Jaylen in a beautiful white dress with sapphires on the waistline up the dress and on her crown. Jaylen's dad walks her down the aisle.

Jaylen stands in front of me, and my dad smiles. "Asland, do you accept Jaylen Ruby Fire-Rose as Luna of the Wolves and Fire Queen of the Phoenixes? Do you promise to rule justly by her side as both as Alpha of the

Wolves and Fire King of the Phoenixes? Do you promise to care for her in sickness and in health for eternal life?" I smile at her, "I do," I say confidently with no doubts in mind. "Jaylen, do you take Asland Mark Johnson as your Fire King of the Phoenixes and Alpha of the Wolves? Do you promise to rule by his side as the Luna of the Wolves and Fire Queen of the Phoenixes and too care for him in sickness and in health for eternal life?" She smiles at me with tears in her eyes, "I do." My father smiles and says his final line. "You can now kiss the bride."

I kiss her and fire surrounds us; no one is surprised by the fire at all anymore. We pull away, and I draw out the sword and kneel in front of my luna and queen. I hold the flaming red sword up to Jaylen. Once in her hands, the flames disappear, revealing a red blade. She kisses the blade and stabs my right shoulder with it. The sword bursts into flames and disappears inside of me. I feel the power of the sword and the power of the minds of the phoenixes. I stand and kiss her again. We dance the first dance, and then it is the father-daughter dance as well as mother-son dance. We eat and, finally, we cut the cake. We talk to everyone and then some of the guests start to load the gifts into my truck. We say our goodbyes and head off to our honeymoon.

Dragon Royalty

It's been five months since my wedding with Asland. Mom will stay the queen until Asland and I have a son to take over the pack. I smile at the thought of a child. "Jay dear, breakfast is ready. Come and eat," Asland says as he walks into the room. I smile and walk with him to the kitchen. I freeze as he opens the door. Instantly, my stomach curls into itself and I run to the nearest bathroom. I throw up multiple times and then Asland walks in. "Are you okay?" he asks as he holds my hair and rubs my back. I glare at him. "Okay, that was a stupid question," he says with an eye roll. After throwing up a few more times, I stop feeling nauseous. I push myself away from the toilet. Asland pulls me into his arms. I lean my head on his chest. Strangely enough, he started to sniff the air. I know he has the nose of a wolf, but does he have to make it obvious that it stinks in here?

He sniffs my neck, and his whole body tenses for just a moment before he launches onto his feet with me in his arms. He smiles and spins me around. I have absolutely no idea what is going on. He looks like a child that has gotten the best gift ever. I can feel his joy,;it is so overwhelming, especially since I have no idea why he is so happy. It's not that I don't like that he is happy, but I literally just threw up and now he is acting like it's the best day in the world. Soon ,his mom and dad run in. "We came as fast as we could," his mom says as Asland sets me down, "Dad. Am I right? Claude says I am, but you went through this twice so can you double check." Right about what? Jersëy nods and walks over. I tense up as he sniffs me. What is going on? He smiles and pats Asland firmly on the shoulder. "Congratulations, my son." I'm so confused, I look to the Luna and she's crying. She runs up and hugs me.

"Oh, I'll finally be a grandma." My eyes go wide at her words. Wait a second, does that mean what I think it does? "Three wolves confirmed it, so I believe it does. We are pregnant," Ruby confirms it. I look toward Asland with tears in my eyes. He smiles back, and he is most likely feeling the joy now running through me. My mother-in-law lets go and I run and hug Asland. He gently holds me and kisses my forehead. "I can't believe that you know I'm pregnant by my scent," I laugh my head off with joy and a hint of embarrassment. "Now, we need to tell my parents. Unlike your parents who can smell it, we actually need to tell the news to mine." I say, and he laughs lightly. "How do you want to do it? Unlike us wolves, you can actually surprise them." This is going to be so fun! "One major problem. We can't shift," Ruby says calmly. I swear that she only shows two emotions- calm and anger. "Hey, I'm very happy to have children. I'm just saying that shifting will harm the child, if not kill it." My eyes widen and I ask Asland, "How are we going to tell them? Ruby says shifting will harm the child."

"Simple- we call them and invite them over for dinner." Asland says, kissing my forehead again. I grab his hand and run to the office where his phone is kept. He never keeps it with him unless he is out of the pack's land. He laughs as he dials my mom's number. "Hello, Asland." I bounce lightly on my feet. He smiles warmly at me, "I'm going to have a pack celebration and I want you, your husband, and your sons to come." There is a long pause before she answers. "We have the dragon royals coming here soon. Would you mind if we brought them? There will only be three." Asland looks to me to deny or accept. I nod for him to accept it. "Of course. See you guys next week." They hang up, and he smiles brightly at me. "I'm going to be a dad!" I can only imagine him wagging his tail in joy.

It's the day of the pack celebration of the new baby, though my family doesn't know what this celebration is for as of yet. I told the pack that's it's a boy, and they asked how I was so certain. I told them that it's because I'm still in human form; if I were to give birth to a girl, I would be in phoenix form, since the shifting gene is only in the girls. The theme is blue, and I'm wearing a light blue dress that is loose on the stomach, even though I'm not showing yet. The pack got me a lot of maternity dresses, even though I told them I could just wear my feathers. However, the looks on their faces shot that idea out the window. The party is being held in and outdoors. Inside in the living room are snacks and drinks, while outside has games and a lot of blue decorations everywhere. I soon hear the beats of wings. I look up and so does the pack. There is my mom; she looks to be carrying three people. One is most likely my dad and, based on the white dot on the man behind, the others are most likely Ashore and his mate Melody. Grandma appears to have Jasper and his mate Iris with her.

Challet is the only one with a phoenix mate, and her name is Maylen. A dragon appears behind them, who also has someone on his back. They all land, and I go to greet them with Asland. The dragon waits until a woman who looks to be a little older than me gets off of him before he shifts. He also appears to be a bit older than me as well, though looks can be deceiving, especially with the supernatural. The lady has a black baby dragon with purple lightening marks all over his body. She sees me and smiles, "Hello. My name is Elizabeth De Drake, Queen of the Dragons, and this is my husband Keyden Andrew De Drake and my son, Dexavier Martin De Drake. Feel free to call me Liz," she says cheerfully. Keyden just nods and turns to my dad. The baby dragon opens his eyes; they are a deep violet. He yawns and stretches out not one but two pairs of wings.

I stare in shock. I have seen a lot of dragons in all different shapes, sizes, and colors, but none with four wings. Liz smiles, "I know, shocking, right? We came to see if the phoenixes can help camouflage or seal his appearance until he is old enough to care for himself. This species of dragon is ultra-rare, even rarer than you, Fire Princess Rubestia. While there has been at least a hundred or so of phoenixes with the white feathers, my son is only the tenth one recorded in history who has four wings. So it's very dangerous for him, especially since my brother in law wants the throne." My eyes widen with all the new information, "How about we discuss that over dinner?" I ask. We all go in to the party. Dexavier seem to have gotten separated from his mom and the little guy climbs up my leg. I pick him up and look around for his mom.

I see her in the distance. I head over, though Asland stops me. "It's time." He pulls me up onto the stage. Dexavier climbs up and lays on my shoulders. Asland now notices him, and he gently pats him on the head. "Don't worry, we'll hand you over to your mom after the announcement." The baby dragon coos. "Aw, he is so cute," I say as we get to the center of the stage. Asland smiles and tips the mic to get everyone's attention. "Pack, family, and friends, we have an announcement, though many may already know." He steps away and opens his arm to me. I walk into them and we say it together. "We are expecting." Everyone erupts into cheers. We step down and return Dexavier to his mom. She smiles, "He is normally fairly shy with new people." Mom comes over and smiles, "Oh, I'm so happy for you, dear." I smile back and hug her. "Shall we do the ritual for this little guy?" I ask as I scratch him under his chin. He coos again; it's so adorable. Liz's eyes widen, "Won't that harm your baby?" I shake my head, "No. I'll be all right. The fire is outside my body for this." She nods, and we go to the training field. My sister-in-law, mom, brothers, and I form a circle around Dexavier. Soon, the black and purple four-winged dragon becomes a pure black two-winged dragon.

ENDINGS ARE BEGINNINGS

I wake up to the crying of our pups. Jaylen starts to get up, but I kiss her forehead and tell her to go back to sleep. I get up and walk into the nursery. I see Crowe asleep next to a crying Raven. I pick up my daughter and rock her back to sleep. She opens her one golden eye and one blue eye. Crowe has the same colors, but he has them in the opposite eyes. Raven and Crowe will be one year old today. I look at Crowe asleep in their metal crib since Raven burned the last two cribs, along with many of my shirts.

I look back at Raven when she starts to cry again, but this time, Crowe starts to cry as well. I try to quiet Raven only for her to burst into flames. Luckily, I don't have a shirt on. The black fire disappears, revealing a black pup. I look at the crib and see another black pup. "Jaylen, love, can you come here." I call out as I look at my two pups. I hear her climb out of bed and walk over. "What is it?" Jaylen asks sleepily. "Our children shifted," I say, looking at Raven in my arms. She is a beautiful black wolf pup with her gold feathers, antennas, and fur diamond on her forehead with black fur wings on her back.

"So, Raven is a phoenix now," Jaylen says happily. "Not quite." I turn and hand her Raven. At first, she looks confused at the black pup, then she smiles. "She's adorable." Jaylen hugs her and kisses her gold diamond. I walk over and pick up my son, who is just a pure black pup with gold and blue eyes. As I pick him up, he wags his tail and sticks out his tongue like any other wolf pup. "Dear, I'm scared, what if the phoenixes don't accept her?" Jaylen asks. I turn and see her holding Raven with tears falling down her face. I smile at her and pull her into a one arm hug. "There's only one way to find out."

The silence is broken by two tiny growls. We both look down at our two pups. Raven playfully bites Crowe's ear as Crowe bites her forepaw. "I think they want to play." I burst out laughing as I set Crowe down on the floor as Jaylen does the some with Raven. Instantly, they start to tackle each other just like normal puppies. I look at my phone and see that it is four in the morning. "I want to play with my pups," Claude whines as we watch them play. I pick both of them up and head to the elevator.

Jaylen follows, and then we go outside. Once outside, I put both pups down on the grass and let Claude have control. He lets them tackle him to the ground and chases them around. Jaylen watches with a large smile on her face. She screams as three wolves tackle her with kisses. She laughs and pushes us away. I lick her face one more time. She chases me with our pups behind her. Claude stops and lets out a powerful howl of joy. Crowe and Raven let out small joyful howls. Jaylen joins the howls with her phoenix call.

At noon, after the twins' nap, we head to Jaylen's parent's house. Raven and Crowe haven't changed back to human form quite yet. Holding on to both the pups and to Jaylen's antennas is hard, but I am able to do it. Jaylen gently glides down to land. I climb down with the pups in my arms. Jaylen shifts and takes Crowe. We walk to the castle and enter. Of course, everyone already knows of Crowe and Raven's existence. We walk to the throne room, but instead of entering, we crack the door open and let Crowe and Raven run in.

Soon, we hear a fit of laughter and then enter. The queen had Crowe licking her face and Raven is being held by the king. "Where did these puppies come from?" We enter with smiles. "They are your grand pups," I say, kneeling down. Raven jumps out of the king's arms and into mine. "Wait, these are Crowe and Raven?" The queen looks at both. "Oh, they are so cute. Especially you, Raven, with your half phoenix look." Raven flaps her tiny wings in happiness with her tail. "She even has wings." The queen walks over with Crowe.

"Yes, mom, we need an anklet for Raven." The queen lets Crowe go, and I let Raven go to play. "So, she shifts like a phoenix and not a werewolf?" We nod and head to the forage with Crowe in the Queen's arms and Raven in mine. "Why in the world would you bring puppies into a forage?" Jasper asks with panic and wide eyes. "Oh, calm down. They have phoenix blood so they will be unharmed," the queen says, putting Crowe down. He walks over to me and whimpers. Raven wakes up and looks down. She starts to wiggle around and whimper. I sigh and set her down. Instantly, they start playing.

"Phoenix blood, how's that?" Ashore asks, looking at the playing pups. "Oh, I don't know, probably because they are your niece and nephew." All three brothers' eyes widen. "I'm a wolf uncle?" Chalet asks, rubbing his neck. I'm about to say something but stop when I see Raven's black flames. "If you haven't noticed, Raven has phoenix traits and we need an anklet so she can shift back." Raven, now a fireball, chases her twin. "We need her first ashes to make it." I roll my eyes and hand him the small bag in my pocket.

Eleven Years Later

It's now been eleven years since Raven got her anklet. Raven and Crowe are now twelve and are inseparable. In fact, it was very hard to separate Raven from Crowe to go to school. Crowe woke up with a fever, which is very high since he's a werewolf with phoenix blood. I shake my head and focus back on my paperwork. I hear the door to my floor open. I turn my head to see little Crowe peeking out of the door. "Crowe, you're supposed to be in bed." His face is red and sweating. "But Daddy, something wrong with Raves." I sigh and kneel down. "Crowe, I know you love Raven and don't like being away, but she's safe and at school."

He madly shakes his head. "No, something really bad happened to her. I heard her, she's scared." Crowe starts to tear up. I sigh, "If I call the school and check on her, will you go back to bed?" Crowe looks about to say no but then nods. I walk to my desk and dial the school's number. It rings for a bit and someone finally answers. "Hello, this is Kelly Jones." I glance at my worried son. "Hello, this is Asland Johnson, I'm calling about my daughter Raven Johnson." I hear typing in the background. "She is in recess right now. Do you want us to get her?"

"No, just checking up on her. Thank you." I hang up and turn to Crowe. "There. She's in recess right now." I pick him up and walk him to his room next to Raven's. I lay him down. "Now go back to sleep." Crowe gives me a scared look and hides under his blanket. Claude grows concerned. I grin and start tickling Crowe. He bursts out laughing. "Sssstttop, daddy." He peeks out from his blanket. "Don't worry. Raven's safe." Crowe nods and closes his eyes. I kiss his forehead and head back to my paperwork. I look at my watch. It is twelve, and I should get something to eat before I finish the paperwork.

After eating a sandwich, I start on my paperwork. After a while, I stretch and yawn. I hate paperwork. My phone rings, and I pick it up. "Hello, this is Alpha Johnson speaking." I hear a scared voice on the other line. "Alpha? Sorry I thought this was Asland Johnson's number." I take a quick glance at my phone. It's the school. Wait, why is the school calling? "Yes, this is Asland. Sorry, I thought you were one of my friends for a second." I let out a forced laugh.

"Asland, I'm sorry to inform you about this, but your daughter appears to be missing." I quickly stand up and run to the elevator. "WHAT DO YOU MEAN MISSING?!" I yell, as Claude comes to the surface at the thought of one of his pups in danger. I hear a freaked out lady answering my question. "It's ten minutes after recess, and she didn't come in at the bell so her teacher went to search for her but only found a gold and amethyst anklet." I growl and throw my phone in anger.

I pound the button on the elevator for the first floor. Once the doors open, I race into my car and drive off like a madman to the school. I race into the office and confront the clerk. She hands me the anklet. I'm guessing she figured out who I am based on my frantic entrance. I smell Raven on the anklet of course, but what angers me more is that it also has a faint rogue scent on it. "Mitchell, get everyone ready. He's back," I mind-link.